I0580031

Mistletoe Kisses

Books by Suzie O'Connell

NORTHSTAR
First Instinct
Mountain Angel
Summer Angel
Twice Shy
Once Burned
Mistletoe Kisses
Starlight Magic
Wild Angel
Forgotten Angel
Last Surrender

TWO-LANE WYOMING
The Road to Garrett

SEA GLASS COVE
The Abalone Shell
The Driftwood Promise

www.suzieoconnell.com

Mistletoe Kisses

A Northstar Novel

SUZIE O'CONNELL

Copyright © 2015 Suzie O'Connell

All rights reserved. No portion of this book may be copied, retransmitted, reposted, duplicated, or otherwise used without the express written approval of the author, except by reviewers who may quote brief excerpts in connection with a review.

This is a work of fiction. Names, characters, places, and incidents are either the product of the author's imagination or used fictitiously, and any resemblance to actual persons, living or dead, business establishments, events, or locales is entirely coincidental.

ISBN-13: 978-1-950813-05-6

For my daughter.
I can't wait to see what dreams inspire your heart.

One

"WHAT THE HELL IS THIS?"

Shannon had to step back to see the tabloid Chris thrust in her face. When he shoved it at her again, she snatched it and pushed past him through the front door into his house. She strode into the kitchen and dropped the paper on the counter. He followed and leaned back against the island with his arms folded tightly across his chest and a dark scowl pinching the features of his usually handsome face. She had hoped he would see the article for what it was. Outright lies. As she noted the fury snapping in his rich green eyes, it was obvious her hope was misplaced.

She lowered her gaze to the cover of the tabloid. There it was, her first brush with the darker side of fame.

Three years she'd been acting and singing on stage without a single *hint* of scandal, and now, less than a week after being offered a role in a movie, the media had targeted her. The title proclaimed, *Quid pro quo? Theatre insider claims actress/singer Shannon O'Neil offered part in film after affair with producer Kevin McNamara.*

Shannon shrugged out of her jacket, hung it on the peg by the pantry, and walked over to the fridge to grab a bottle of water with methodical movements.

"Are you going to answer me?" Chris asked.

"Not when you're acting like this."

"How should I act, Shannon?"

"You actually believe that?" She jabbed the bottle toward the tabloid.

"It's pretty damning, don't you think? I used to think you were this sweet, innocent girl, but now I know you're just a lying, cheating whore."

She jerked back and stared at him. She was a *what?* Taking a deep breath, she smoothed her features. Getting defensive would only make this worse. "Can we talk about this when you've had time to calm down and think and realize it's a fabrication?"

"I've been thinking about it all day, Shannon, and a lot of things are starting to make sense. Like how an entirely unknown high school music and drama teacher was miraculously offered a starring role in a musical."

"The director was a friend of my drama professor. You know that, Chris."

He continued as if she hadn't spoken. "No, not one

starring role. Role after *starring* role. There are a lot of things I've been willing to overlook, but I can't forgive this."

"Forgive *what*, Chris? It's not true! They took a picture at the exact right time to make it look like something it wasn't, and then they wrote a lie about it. And what *things* are you willing to over look? There is *nothing*."

"How about your obsession with that Montana college football team? I always wondered if there was something more to it than what you told me. You've got a thing for the quarterback, don't you? The blond kid— your brother's friend. And let's not forget that kiss with your friend Ty when we visited your brother for Christmas that year. Oh, no, we can't leave that out. That's the most damning one because I saw it with my own eyes. Makes me wonder what you do on your solo trips out to Montana, you little slut."

"Oh, for crying out loud, Chris! Luke is a friend of my family's and that kiss with Ty under the mistletoe was two years ago." Tumultuous anger and helplessness trembled through her, threatening to break free. Why didn't he believe her? "It meant *nothing*. I apologized for it, and Ty apologized for it."

"Nothing? I know what I saw, Shannon. And your face and your eyes right now confirm it."

Her hand twitched, wanting to slap that smug sneer off his face. Tears burned her eyes, but flaring anger held them back. "It was an *accident*. He didn't mean to—"

"Bullshit, Shannon."

"Three things," she said. Her voice cracked. "Three *misconceptions*. That's all you can come up with and you call me a slut?"

"That's more than I *need* to come up with. More than I should be *able* to come up with. You slept with another man. A married man at that." He let go of her gaze for a moment to stare into the distance. The muscle in his jaw twitched as he clenched and unclenched his teeth. Finally, he returned his eyes to her and said very softly, "Get out of my house."

"Chris, please don't do this."

"I said… get out of my house. I'm done with you."

"Can we please talk about this?"

"There's nothing more to talk about."

"Yes, there is. You're being a jealous ass and there's no reason at all for you to be jealous."

"I am well over being jealous. Please leave."

The quiet, firm resolve with which he spoke those final words cut more deeply than any amount of railing fury could have.

"I hope you feel like crap when you realize how wrong you are."

With her tears spilling over, Shannon yanked her coat off the rack and ran to the front door without looking back. She slammed the door behind her as she stepped back out into the black November night. Rain pelted her as she dashed to her car, but she didn't care. It was as if the sky was crying with her.

She and Chris had planned to have a quiet,

romantic dinner after her meeting with her agent. Instead, the tabloid had been waiting for her when she'd walked into Macie's sleek office overlooking the Seattle waterfront. How she had missed it after spending all day in the mall with her mom doing a little early Christmas shopping, she had no idea, but she had, and seeing herself on the cover had taken the wind out of her. She recalled falling into the cushy chair across the desk from Macie, unable to take her eyes off the image or the headline. Macie didn't believe it and said she was already in damage control mode, but Shannon had barely heard her agent's voice.

Her first thought had been of Chris and of what he would think. With the naïveté she still somehow managed to cling to, she had believed he loved her enough to trust her and to know it was all a hideous fallacy, but there had been a voice in the back of her mind that remembered how he'd reacted to the way Ty Evans had kissed her in Northstar. The memory of that kiss was, two years later, still as sharp as if it had happened this morning.

"Come on, Shy Eyes, it's my birthday. And look," Ty had said. "We're standing under the mistletoe. You *have* to kiss me."

Sure enough, hanging from the branded beam in the restaurant of her brother and sister-in-law's inn was a sprig of mistletoe. She had intended to give him only a simple kiss on the cheek, between friends, but he'd turned his face at the last second, and rather than stubble-roughened cheek, she'd met with soft, seeking lips. She had meant to pull away and teasingly chastise him, but instead she'd lingered, intrigued and surprised by the flare of heat and the way her heart had jumped erratically in her chest. When they'd pulled apart moments later, she'd caught a brief glimpse of vulnerability and desire in his blue eyes that ignited a thousand questions she didn't dare answer. To search for the answers might have changed their friendship, added a jarring awkwardness to what had—until that moment—been among the easiest, most uncomplicated relationships in her life.

Chris had returned from the restroom just in time to see the kiss. He'd been angry at first, but fury had soon slipped into sulking jealousy. Ty had apologized the next day, saying that he'd had a little too much to drink that night—a lie. Ty didn't drink, but Shannon didn't figure it would be wise to mention that. Chris had acted like he was appeased, and she had thought he had forgiven the incident.

Clearly not.

Tonight was not the first time he'd brought it up, either. He'd mentioned it a couple times to guilt her into forgoing an evening out with Kevin and Macie and few other friends and calling off the solo trip to see Pat and Aelissm she had planned to make this spring. Shannon momentarily thought of her brother's deceased ex-fiancée. The fact that she was even remotely reminded of that manipulative, abusive bitch was enough to stop her tears. If Chris didn't believe her and if he wouldn't give her the chance to prove her innocence, she had no room in her life for him. It was sure to be more easily vowed than upheld, but even that temporary resolution was better than nothing.

When she pulled into the ferry terminal and parked to wait for the next boat to Bainbridge Island, she picked up the copy of the tabloid she'd left sitting on the passenger seat. The article was accompanied by a picture of her with Kevin McNamara, a good friend of the man who had directed five of the seven plays in which she'd starred. She'd hit it off immediately with the wealthy theatre and film producer and counted him among her close friends, but the idea that they'd had an affair was preposterous. Unfortunately, she couldn't tell Chris or anyone else why because it wasn't her secret to tell, and he probably wouldn't believe her even if it were; he'd never liked Kevin, whose touchy-feely tendencies added brevity to the story.

She sighed. The photograph was almost a month old and showed her and Kevin embracing outside the theatre after the overwhelmingly successful opening night of their most recent production. He had kissed her on the cheek, but the photographer had snapped the shot half a moment before, and with the angle and poor lighting, it looked like Kevin was going in for a full-on-the-mouth kiss. The caption below it read, *Silver-voiced Shannon O'Neil and philanthropist theatre and film mogul Kevin McNamara stealing a quick kiss after the sold-out opening performance of "Stars Over Seattle."*

"They can all rot," she muttered, dropping the

tabloid onto the passenger seat with the cover down so she couldn't see it. She choked on a renewed threat of tears.

She pushed the article and every other thought out of her mind for the time being. The gentle rolling of the ferry as it crossed the stormy Puget Sound was soothing, and she let herself be lulled into a half-sleeping stupor. Disinclined to be around any people at all, she took the less traveled, winding rural roads home to Kingston, and the darkness was as calming as the ferry ride had been. The peace she found lasted until she parked in front of her house. She climbed the stairs, and after she stepped inside, she leaned against the closed door for a moment.

"You're home early," her roommate remarked from her customary reading bench beside the big bay window overlooking the harbor.

"Yeah," Shannon replied and tossed the tabloid at her friend.

"I already saw this. I'm assuming Chris took it like an asshole."

"That's one way to put it."

"Then he doesn't deserve you."

"Thanks."

Shannon wandered into the kitchen. She should eat something, even if she only heated up leftovers. Not that she was hungry. Celeste joined her and regarded her with worried brown eyes that reminded Shannon of a doe.

"You all right?"

"I don't know what I am. My boyfriend of three

years just broke up with me over a lie. I know I should either be angry or heartbroken or *something*, but right now, I just feel… empty."

"Oh, honey." Celeste hugged her. "Well, this might cheer you up. Your brother called about twenty minutes ago."

The corner of Shannon's lips lifted in a hint of a smile. She could use a trip to Northstar right now, even if she only visited in her mind. So, while Celeste set about cooking dinner for them both, Shannon took the cordless into the living room and dialed her brother's number.

"I didn't expect you to call me back so quickly," came Pat's cherished voice. "How are you?"

There was a note of concern in his voice that told her he wasn't making a general inquiry, which meant he knew about the article. Their parents must have called him and told him already.

"I'll let you know when I figure it out."

"Aelissm wanted me to tell you to kick the writers of the article in the balls if you get the chance. I tend to agree with her."

Shannon let out a bark of laughter. "If that's all it would take to solve the problem, I would. Unfortunately, I don't think that would change Chris's mind."

"He believes this garbage?"

"It seems so." She repeated her conversation with her now ex-boyfriend, leaving out certain terms that were sure to infuriate him, and Pat listened quietly.

"You don't seem too upset."

"Maybe I'm in shock, but his attitude tonight…. Sorry to dredge up old memories, but he reminded me a little of the bitch."

"Nine years later, you still call her that."

"If the name fits…."

"True enough. Will you be all right?"

"I think I'll be okay once the dust settles."

"If you need to get away for a while, you're always welcome here, and we'd love to see you."

The offer was very tempting, but she politely declined. She had the film deal—though production didn't start until March *if* she decided to sign the contract; at the moment, she wanted to turn it down—and a couple of upcoming plays she was very interested in. Plus, Kevin had some contacts in the music business that were interested in her. Like her father and his father, music was in her soul, and while the stage and silver screen had a tantalizing pull, it was singing and songwriting that she wanted most.

Time. I need some time to think about all this.

"I'd really love to see you guys, too. And since Mom and Dad are headed out that way for Christmas… maybe I *should* come."

"That would be wonderful. Think about it and let me know what you decide. I've gotta run. The Conners just arrived for cards."

"Don't have too much fun."

"Not possible. I love you, Shannon."

"I love you, too, Pat."

She ended the call and turned to find Celeste standing in the doorway between the kitchen and living room, holding two plates of creamy, mouthwatering pasta and staring at her with a quizzical frown.

"Go ahead and say it," Shannon said. "I can take it from you."

"Say what?"

"That this kind of crap is what comes with even the tiniest bit of fame."

Celeste shook her head and several strands of her lustrous dark hair tumbled loose from her sloppy ponytail. "That's not at all what I was going to say. We've been friends for—what, seven years now?—since we were first paired up in that ridiculously tiny dorm room, which means I know you pretty well, right?"

"Better than anyone outside of my immediate family and Ty."

"Remind me. What does Ty call you?"

"Shy Eyes."

"Exactly. So—and don't answer this right now—since this kind of crap is likely to become the norm if you continue down this path to fame and fortune, how badly do you want to keep acting and singing?"

Shannon took the plate and silverware Celeste handed her and sat on the window bench with her feet tucked under her. Her roommate sat in the armchair a few feet away.

"All right. I get it." Shannon gestured at the tabloid lying beside her on the bench. "If that is what I'll have to endure, maybe this isn't the career for me. But you forget that I didn't exactly like teaching, either."

"I remember that you liked teaching well enough, and that you were good at it like your dad, but you were in a large school with too many students and a miniscule budget and the expectation that you could work miracles."

Shannon growled. "What's your point? That I should trade a career I usually enjoy and that pays pretty damned well for one that frustrates me and doesn't pay squat?"

"My point is that maybe you should take a step back and let yourself have a good-old-fashioned mid-twenties identity crisis. Give yourself a few weeks or a couple months away from everything and take a look at what you want *deep* in your heart. Ask yourself if you want the acting and music enough to put up with the crap that comes with it."

"Just because of one tabloid article."

"An article that ended a three-year relationship with the decisiveness of a guillotine. And don't tell me you aren't thinking about taking a break. I heard the longing in your voice when you told Pat you wanted to visit for Christmas."

"I can't just drop everything and run away to Montana."

"Says who? You have enough money saved to take at least a six-month sabbatical, the last show of your play is in six days, and if you're worried about the movie deal, the producer is a good friend who I'm sure will give you other chances." Celeste wiggled her eyebrows. "Maybe you could make nice with Ty while you're there."

Shannon rolled her eyes. "I can't just up and leave, Celeste."

"When was the last time you took a break? You've been going balls to the wall since you graduated from high school, missy, so maybe it's time for a vacation. Listen to your heart *before* your mind has time to override it. What is it telling you?"

With a sigh, Shannon replied, "That a trip to Northstar right now sounds absolutely splendid."

* * *

"I hear Shannon O'Neil is coming for a visit," Heather remarked as Ty loped past where she sat on the top rail of the corral.

He spared her only a glance, afraid anything more would reveal how much the news intrigued him. She'd spoken rather loudly—certainly loud enough to be heard over the rhythmic thuds of his mount's hooves—so he sincerely doubted she would think he hadn't caught what she'd said. He liked Heather. With long, rich brown hair, confident blue eyes, a strong-featured face, and an athletic body, she was undeniably attractive. Even more than her physical beauty, Ty appreciated her quick wit and her unabashed readiness to speak her mind. At twenty-two— four years his junior—she had a surprising poise and self-assuredness. And yet, the mere mention of Pat O'Neil's little sister had his heart tripping in his chest. Heather, with all her charms, couldn't make it do that.

"She's supposed to be here tonight," she added on his next pass.

Shannon in Northstar again, Ty thought. *Looks like Christmas is coming early this year.*

Though he talked to her every week, he hadn't seen her since he'd given in to impulse and kissed her under the mistletoe. He'd started a fire with that kiss and had not yet found a way to put it out. Neither of them had spoken of it after he'd apologized to her boyfriend for his trespass, and though he was fairly certain she'd felt the spark, time and distance made him doubt. She had been out only once since to spend a long weekend with her brother and his family last summer, but Ty had been in Bozeman at a competition, so he hadn't yet had an opportunity to see if the kiss was a fluke or if there was something more between them. The blue ribbon he'd won hadn't come close to making up for missing her visit, but his family and their small ranch and horse-training operation had benefited from the substantial boost his reputation had received as a result.

If Shannon was coming to Northstar....

"She might be here already."

Ty frowned and, with his hands resting on his thighs, lifted his left leg away from his horse's barrel while pressing his right closer. The piebald mare pivoted to the left. She stopped immediately and walked toward Heather when he squeezed gently with both legs. He was genuinely impressed with the young mare, all the more because the man he'd bought her from had claimed she was "untrainable." Quite the opposite, Ty now knew, more glad than ever that he'd obeyed the compulsion to buy her. She was one of the most eager and willing horses he'd ever had the pleasure to work with.

"Whoa," he murmured as he relaxed both legs and sat straighter. She stopped before the command died on his lips, further pleasing him. He leaned forward over her neck, stroking his hands over her thick winter coat and scratching vigorously along her mane. "Good girl, Holly."

"You amaze me, Ty. My dad's damned good with horses, and yours is even more so, but you are truly gifted. She loves this."

Ty nodded his thanks, then tilted his head and studied his girlfriend with narrowed eyes. "What's on your mind, Heather? For a woman who rivals my mother in the department of bluntness, you're being awfully cryptic."

"Cryptic? How am I being—"

"There's a reason you mentioned Shannon. What is it?"

Heather brushed her fingertips over Holly's velvety nose for a moment before she answered. "I think it's time we call it quits. Dating, I mean. I know you want to start settling down, maybe think about starting a family, and… I'm just not ready for that yet."

Ty ducked his gaze for a moment, though he wasn't surprised. "What brought this on?"

"Mostly the way you've been acting around your sister and her brood. When I heard Shannon's on her way, something clicked. I know you love her, Ty, and I may regret this in a few years because you're a great guy, but you may have a chance to start something with her, and I don't want to be the one to screw that up."

Unable to meet the confidence in her eyes, Ty turned his gaze east toward the tall granite peaks of the Northstar Mountains. They were blocked from his view by the forest-crowned ridge sheltering the bowl in which the corrals, barns, and lower pasture sat, and he wished he could see them. This late in the afternoon with the cool shadows lengthening, they would be bathed in sharp golden light.

"Shannon has a boyfriend," he said.

"You're not going to try to talk me out of this?"

It almost—*almost*—sounded like she wanted him to. "Is there any point in trying?"

"No," she answered. "As to Shannon, I'm pretty sure she *had* a boyfriend."

"What makes you think that's changed?" He returned his attention to her.

"Oh please, Ty. She's never come out here without at least two months' notice. I heard Aelissm say this morning that she just up and decided to visit only a week or so ago. Right as her acting career is set to rocket into the stratosphere. Does that sound like everything is still all sunshine and rainbows to you?"

Ty didn't dare hope Heather was right. Shannon

had complained more than once that Chris seemed to be taking his sweet time moving their relationship in a more lasting direction, but the man would have to be dense to let go of a woman like Shannon. Hell, Ty was probably a fool for letting Heather slip away without a fight, but she—like Shannon—was much like the horses he trained; the best results always came when they *wanted* to work with him. Unlike horses, however, women were not nearly so easily won over. It had taken little more than sugary treats, some sweet-talking, and patience to get Holly to follow him around like a faithful shadow.

"Are you okay?" Heather asked.

"I…. Yeah. I guess so. I mean, we aren't—weren't—all that serious, anyhow."

"Right. Barely more than friends with benefits. Although, there is one benefit I still want."

"And that is?"

"I still want you to teach me all your training tricks. That is, if it wouldn't be too awkward…."

Ty smiled. "I can't make any promises about the awkward part, but I'm glad you want to keep learning. I might be looking for some extra help before too much longer, and so far, you're my best hope."

"Ah gee, thanks, Ty. Need me to help with anything else tonight?"

"No, I can manage."

"All right. Hey. Thanks for not making a big deal about this."

All he could do was nod and watch her saunter

away. Ty nudged Holly over to the corral gate and leaned down to slip the rope loop off the post. He pushed the gate open with his foot, then guided his horse through with the lightest squeeze of his legs. Damn, she was a great horse. He had an idea about entering her in a competition he was sure her former owner was sure to attend just to shove it in the prick's face that he'd sold a gem.

"Stubborn, stupid, and worthless mare my ass," Ty said, fondly patting her shoulder. "Intelligent, loyal, and champion mare are much more fitting terms for you, aren't they, Holly?"

She flicked her ears, listening intently to his every word. He curled his fingers around a fistful of her black mane and tightened his legs a little more. She moved effortlessly into a ground-eating lope up the trail to the ridge crest, her hooves crunching and squeaking in the snow. The brisk November air stung his exposed face, but he reveled in it, thrilled by the freedom of riding bareback without a bridle through the wintry landscape, truly in tune with his horse, and elated by the hope that Shannon would soon be in Northstar.

When they reached the crown of the ridge, he relaxed his legs, cuing Holly to slow to a walk and finally to a stop just as the mountains came into view through the trees. The sight of the Northstar Mountains alight with the late afternoon sunlight was nothing short of breathtaking. The forests of lodgepole pine and Douglas fir that blanketed the shoulders of the peaks were still heavily dusted with the snow that had fallen last night, and the contrast between the white mountains, white hayfields, and the dark green of the pines and firs was muted. Even the leafless, red-brown branches of the scrub willows gathered along the many creeks of the valley wore thick coats of white.

Ty had lived here his entire life, born right here on the Bar E Ranch in the middle of a Christmas Eve snowstorm, and the beauty of this place never failed to leave him awestruck. He couldn't imagine living anywhere else, and he wondered what it would take to convince Shannon to stay here in Northstar. He knew she liked it here, and he had hoped since meeting her—and especially since kissing her—that she would realize this could be her home like it was now her brother's.

With a sigh, Ty again patted Holly's neck. He noted a restlessness settling over him, and he wanted keep riding, but he'd already put Holly through a pretty good workout this afternoon. Besides, it was getting on toward dinnertime. As he rode back to the ranch compound at a leisurely trot, he pondered his lack of concern over Heather's decision to end their relationship. Was he really okay with it or was the promise of seeing Shannon again just that powerful? Both, he decided. He and Heather had been dating only a month, and he hadn't moved very far beyond seeing her as only his friend. The term lover, though accurate enough, didn't fit right. Shannon, on the other hand, had captivated him from the moment they'd first been introduced at Pat and Aelissm's wedding. Over the years, he had been content to keep Shannon as a friend despite the nagging desire for more because he wanted her in his life and he hadn't cared how.

Memories he'd collected of her occupied his mind as he groomed and fed Holly and finished the rest of his evening chores. When he reached his cabin, he stoked the fire in his wood stove and walked into the kitchen. He stood there for a few minutes, aware that he was hungry but not feeling much like cooking. Instead of starting dinner, he grabbed his truck keys. He didn't think about where he was going or why, trusting his heart to figure it out, but he wasn't in the least surprised when he pulled up in front of the squat A-frame with dark brown siding and crisp white trim that was the restaurant of the Bedspread Inn. The big windows and glass doors of the front wall brightly reflected the scene behind him, and he stared over his shoulder at the mountains for a moment before climbing out of his truck. The light was now rosy and reminded him vividly of that evening two years ago.

He started toward the stairs up to the inn's restaurant, but stopped in his tracks when he noticed the SUV he'd parked beside. It had Washington plates. His heart did that skittery thing again, and he took the steps two at a time.

Ty stepped into the dining room, glanced as he always did at the dark beam with his family's brand emblazoned in bright teal. Heat radiated from the roaring fire in the stone hearth that dominated the center of the room. At first, the restaurant appeared to be empty, but he heard voices. Then Pat's striking blonde wife peeked around the fireplace, saw him, and grinned.

"I believe there's someone here who'd love to see you, Shannon," Aelissm remarked.

If he had worried her recent successes in the spotlight had changed her somehow, he'd been wrong. She was just how he remembered, from the gentle waves of dark auburn hair that cascaded over her shoulders to the dancing, innocent hazel eyes smiling at him from that softly beautiful face. She was every bit as alluring as he recalled, slender with feminine curves and, dressed in a slim-fitting maroon sweater and jeans, more shyly comfortable than brazenly sexy. Shannon O'Neil was the classic girl-next-door and exactly what Ty wanted in a woman.

"Ty," she murmured, walking slowly toward him.

"Hey there, Shy Eyes." He met her halfway, concerned when she didn't wrap him in her usual enthusiastic hug. There was a haze of sadness in her eyes, he noted. "What's wrong?"

"It's been a long week," she replied. Finally, she embraced him and whispered, "It's so good to see you."

Ty closed his eyes and held her tightly, delighted to have her in his arms but wondering if it was real. Two hours ago, he had been dating Heather with no idea when he'd see Shannon again, and now he was single and she was here.

She leaned back to look at him. "What? Aren't you glad to see me, too?"

A slow, tender smile curved his lips. "You bet I

am."

She hugged him again.

"Join me for dinner?"

"I think I'm going to have to pass tonight, Ty. I'm exhausted."

"No offense, but I'm going to have to agree about that. You *look* tired, and I'll bet the roads were a mess. Why didn't you wait until they cleared a little? This is kind of a spur-of-the-moment trip, and you're not usually so impulsive."

"I got my first taste of what it's like to catch the attention of the tabloids. Chris took the writer of the article's word over mine. So… here I am."

"He broke up with you?"

She only nodded and lowered her eyes.

"Is he stupid?"

She let out a derisive sniff but said nothing.

"Are you all right?"

"Not really. Which is why I'm here."

"I'm here for you if you need it."

"I know you are, but right now, I think I just need some time to clear my head. I am a little upset with men in general right now, and I don't want to take that out on you."

That stung a little, though he wasn't sure why. To hide it, he joked, "What about Pat?"

"He's my brother. He *has* to put up with me."

"And I'm your friend. I'm pretty sure helping you weather the storm is one of the stipulations in our friendship contract."

At last, she met his gaze again and smiled. It didn't touch her eyes, but it was better than nothing. "Give me a week or so, and I'll stop by the Bar E. I want to meet this horse you're so smitten with. Just… give me a little space for now, okay? We'll have plenty of time to catch up once I relax a little."

"How long are you planning to stay?"

"I was thinking I'd stick around until the day after New Years. Maybe longer. I don't know yet. I'm sort of winging it on this trip."

"Just give me a call when you want to meet Holly."

With a nod, Shannon turned toward the back of the restaurant and called out to her sister-in-law. "I'll see you and Pat in a little while."

Aelissm reappeared. "Heading up to the cabin?"

"Yeah. I should probably take a nap before you unleash my niece and nephews on me."

"See you in a couple hours, then."

Shannon laid her hand on Ty's arm for a moment and squeezed, then brushed passed him and out the door. He stared after her, fighting the urge to follow. She needed space right now.

"Shall I break out the mistletoe early this year?" Aelissm inquired.

When he turned his attention to her, he found her grinning broadly at him. "Depends. Do you think Pat would shoot me if I asked to date his sister?"

Two

"YOU DON'T HAVE to do this, Shannon. You're more than welcome to stay with us."

Shannon settled her sacks of groceries on the kitchen table in John and Tracie Hammond's rental cabin and faced her brother with a placating smile. "I know I'm welcome, but I also know that your cabin is cramped enough with three kids, especially now that Seth has hit the terrible threes. A week was more inconvenience than I need to put on your family."

"You're never an inconvenience. Aeli and I love having you home, and the kids enjoy having you around to grant their every whim."

She laughed softly and studied Pat's cherished face, pleased to note that the strain Sara Montgomery had wrought from him and made him look older than his years was long gone, replaced by a few faint lines of mirth and happiness. *I could thank Aelissm every day for bringing my big brother back, and it wouldn't be enough.* "You can stop trying to convince me you aren't relieved this cabin came open and that I won't have to camp out on your couch for the next month and a half. Or however long I stay this time."

Standing on her toes, she wrapped her arms around Pat's neck and sighed. She briefly considered a wise crack about him hogging the genes for height from their father and leaving so few for her, but she was too glad for his soothing presence.

"It's okay, Pat. We'll still have more time together and see more of each other than we've had since that last summer before I graduated from college."

"So we will." He gestured to the groceries. "Want a hand putting these away?"

"Sure… if you don't need to get home to Aeli and the kids."

"They'll understand."

As they stashed her purchases, they talked about the goings-on of Northstar, a place that was as much her home now as Kingston, where she lived with Celeste, and North Bend, where she and Pat had grown up in the shadow of the Cascade Mountains. With an age difference of eleven years, they hadn't actually shared much of their childhoods, and perhaps because of that, they had an effortless, affectionate relationship. Pat's innate gentleness *made* it so, and from the beginning, she'd always known he would listen to her worries and soothe them away. That tenderness and sensitivity, which she was infinitely relieved to see had only been bruised by the bitch, was something Chris lacked—a realization she had come to only after his reaction to the tabloid.

Ty has it, though, which is probably why we hit it off so well the first time we met. Her lips twisted in chagrin and amusement. *Probably what keeps our friendship strong even when we're apart for months or years at a time.*

Suddenly, Shannon wanted to see him. For a week now, she'd been putting off a visit with him with the belief that she needed some time alone to get her heart straightened out again.

Maybe Chris was right to be jealous.

"So, when are you planning to go see Ty?" Pat inquired lightly. "Because he's been asking about you, and I'm tired of telling him you're still settling in."

Shannon laughed more loudly this time. "Have you picked up mind reading from June? Because I was just thinking of heading over there as soon as we're done here."

"It was pretty obvious. You were staring through the back of the cabin toward the Bar E like you could see through walls." He flipped her ponytail over her shoulder like he had countless times when she was younger, a subtle gesture to let her know he worried about her. "Why have you been avoiding him? And don't try to lie and say you haven't. I know you too well, sis."

"I keep thinking of that day he kissed me two years ago. I've tried not to let it become an issue between us, but there are so many questions, and after Chris brought it up as one of the reasons why I'm a…." She stuffed her hands in her pockets and scowled. It still stung.

Pat's expression darkened to match hers. "Do you have any idea how much that pissed me off? It's a good thing he's in Washington."

Shannon studied her brother for a moment. When she'd told him the day after she'd arrived exactly what Chris had said to her, she'd glimpsed a flare of the same chilling anger that she'd seen in his eyes only when Sara had had her talons in him. More than a little unnerved by those memories, she shut them out and glanced toward the Bar E again. "Why did he do it?"

"Because he's an idiot?"

"Not Chris. Ty. Unless you're calling Ty an idiot for kissing me."

"I was talking about Chris. Whether or not Ty was an idiot remains to be seen, but I'd say he's pretty sharp."

Drumming her fingers on her arm, she shifted her gaze back to Pat and frowned. "Why did he kiss me like that? Did he *mean* to kiss me on the lips, or was it an accident? Did I hesitate too long, and he was only looking to see why?"

"Maybe it's time you asked him."

Her frown deepened.

"I do know one thing, though. He has a talent for making you smile that Chris never figured out." Pat draped an arm around her shoulders and tucked her into his side. "Put the questions away for now, have a good visit with Ty, and let him put you in a better mood before I see you again. If he can do that, I won't mind if you're a little late for dinner."

She unfolded her arms and hugged him tightly again. With their chore finished, she walked with him to the door.

"See you at six-thirty," she called as he trotted down the stairs of the broad deck.

He gave her a wink before he climbed into his truck. "Six-thirty-*ish*."

She closed the door after he drove away and inspected the cabin while she debated driving or walking over to Ty's. She'd been in the cabin several times before—she and her parents and Chris had stayed in it over Christmas the year Ty had kissed her—and she'd always loved the open layout and cozy loft.

There were some new additions. Poster-sized photographs had replaced the generic cowboy-themed prints that had adorned the walls on her last visit, and she was certain the photographer was Skye Hammond. Closer inspection of the one on the wall behind the couch confirmed it; it was a shot Skye had taken during her initial stay in Northstar of the Lazy H hay-stacking crew. Back when she'd still been Skye Hathaway. Shannon instantly recognized John Hammond and his sons Nick, Aaron, and Henry. Ben and Luke Conner were in the box while her own brother raked hay clear of the beaverslide's pulleys.

A deep, fond smile warmed her face. Coming to Northstar to regroup was a brilliant idea. So was a long walk through snowy woods and pastures, so she kicked off her showier, knee-high black boots and stuffed her feet into the faux fur-lined snow boots she'd bought on her first full day back in Montana. With her head protected by a knit hat, her body hugged by a bulky parka, and her hands snuggled into thick mittens, she stepped out the kitchen door into the chilly November afternoon and tromped down the metal grate ramp.

The half-mile trek took her through the bare-branched aspen grove behind the cabin, across a tiny creek flowing too quickly to freeze solid, up over a ridge speckled with sagebrush half-buried beneath pillows of snow, and into the dense band of Douglas fir and spruce clustered on the north-facing slope. The snow beneath the sheltering boughs was thinner than elsewhere, and she was able to make better time unhindered by the knee-deep, ice-crusted, and shifting powder. Just beyond the trees, a narrow road descended from the higher pasture that sprawled over the sagebrush hills and up the side of the ridge that sheltered the narrow valley where Pat and Aelissm's cabin was located. Where the ranch road met the faint trail from the Hammonds' rental cabin, it snaked through willow-choked creek bottom to a gate in the fence of the Bar E's lower pasture. She traipsed along the tracks made by one of the Evanses' ranch trucks toward the barn, pavilion, and corrals where Ty would surely still be working.

Compared to other spreads in the Northstar Valley such as the Lazy H and C-Diamond ranches that sprawled over thousands of acres, the Bar E was small at just over eight hundred sixty acres, and the bulk of the Evanses' income came from breeding and training horses rather than cattle, something that made the ranch's security tenuous in this age of technology and increased use of mechanical equipment. Still, Ty's father had made a name for himself, and Ty was well on his way to surpassing his sire in horsemanship.

The reason why was crystal clear as the corral on the near side of the barn came into view. Ty was, as she'd figured, working with one of his horses with neither saddle nor bridle and directing the pretty piebald mare with such subtle cues that Shannon had no hope of seeing how he did it. As the horse spun, changed leads on the fly, or shifted from a ground-eating lope to a lazy walk, Ty rode like he was an extension of the mare. The strength and balance he exhibited was phenomenal. With blue eyes alight with the soul-deep pride and pleasure of his work, his brown hair peeking out from beneath his black cowboy hat, and his lanky but powerful body clad in the quintessential cowboy get-up—Wrangler jeans, a green and black plaid wool shirt, and well worn Carhartt coat—he was boldly sexy.

Breathtaking, Shannon corrected, watching him from the shadow of the big Doug fir a dozen feet away from the gate of the corral. Putting Ty and sexy in the same sentence made her squirm. He was her best friend, and therefore she should *not* be thinking of him in those terms. *But he is… and I am. And I have been since that damned kiss.*

Pat was right. She needed to ask about it, but watching Ty was so much easier and so much more enjoyable than broaching the uncomfortable subject, so she allowed him to distract her for several minutes more. At last, the desire to not only observe him but also interact with him drove her from the shade of the tree.

"You'd think after all this time I wouldn't still be so mesmerized by how truly gifted you are at training horses," she greeted as he trotted past.

The black and white horse slid to a stop with no visible cue Shannon could discern, and Ty beamed. "I keep trying to tell you. The secret isn't in the training. It's showing them that they can trust me over their instincts to flee."

"However you do it, it's amazing."

He slid off the horse's back, and as he opened the gate to let Shannon in, his smile softened. He embraced her, and she nearly sighed in contentment.

"I'm glad you're finally here, Shy Eyes. I was beginning to wonder if I'd get to see you again before you went back to Washington."

She opened her mouth to remind him she'd be here until at least New Years, then snapped it shut. "Sorry, Ty. I haven't been in the best mood, and I didn't want to take that out on you."

"So you said last Saturday, but I'd rather endure your grumpiness than go on missing you. Especially when you're so close you could probably hear me if I yelled loud enough."

The wall of ice Chris's callous words had formed around her heart splintered, and she leaned into Ty and let the solid warmth of him melt away some more of it. Pat was right about that, too. Ty *did* have a gift for improving her mood simply by occupying the same space with her, and it likely came from the same natural serenity that made her brother so easy to trust and open up to—the same gentleness that was the heart of Ty's remarkable ability to get a horse do whatever he asked.

With her arm tucked around his waist, Shannon turned toward the beautiful black and white paint, who stood a few paces away with her head lifted and her ears forward in an unmistakable display of curiosity and interest. She had such alert, intelligent eyes, and Shannon reached her hand toward the horse. After only a moment's hesitation to sniff it, the mare stepped closer and pressed her velvety nose into her palm. At the invitation, Shannon smoothed her hand over the horse's face, then scratched around her ears.

"I'm guessing this is your new love Holly," she murmured, delighted when the pretty animal relaxed and leaned into her touch. "The supposedly untrainable horse."

"This is my Holly," Ty confirmed. He stepped away to run his hands over the mare's thick winter coat, down her neck and chest to her knee. He gently tapped just below the joint, then laid his hand on her nose and pushed it in toward her chest ever so slightly. Obediently, Holly folded one leg, tucked her nose close in beside her knee, and rocked her body back into a full bow.

Shannon grinned. "You need to make her last owner eat his words at the earliest opportunity. She's incredible, Ty."

"I've been thinking that, too. He needs to see that it wasn't the horse but him who needs the training." Ty slid his hand under Holly's jaw and pressed up. The mare straightened again.

"It's almost like magic, what you do. I need to get a video of you at work and show it to Kevin. He didn't believe me when I told him about you."

He lifted a brow at her. "Kevin McNamara? How did I come up in a conversation with *him*?"

"I've talked to him about you a lot, actually, and more lately because the role in his movie will require a lot of riding."

"Didn't you say it was some kind of fantasy, like *Lord of the Rings*?"

"Yep."

"Want to ride her?"

"But… she has no saddle or bridle."

"So? You've ridden bareback before. More times than I can remember."

"Yeah, but not with out a bridle. And that was when I was out here for months at a time and we went riding every day. I haven't been on a horse since...." *Since the day you kissed me.* She didn't say it out loud.

"Are you saying you haven't been on a horse since the last time you were out here?"

She nodded.

"But that was two years ago, Shy Eyes. What about Celeste's horses? Don't you girls ever ride them anymore?"

"They were getting too old to ride even then... and anyhow, she and I have both been too busy with work."

"In that case, you have to ride Holly. Right now. And we'll go riding every day together while you're here, just like old times. Can't have you saying you can ride and then making a fool of yourself in front of the director." Ty winked and folded his gloved hands together beside Holly, forming a cradle to help Shannon onto the horse's back.

She didn't tell him she was seriously considering turning down the offer. With the blissful memories of their summers together tantalizing her, now didn't seem like the right time to talk about it even though she wanted to get his thoughts on the matter. She put her foot into the cradle of his hands and swung her leg over the paint's back as he lifted her so effortlessly that she nearly overbalanced. She *was* out of practice. Still, the hand up, the conversation about horses.... It was all so wonderfully familiar—a routine they'd gone through together hundreds if not thousands of times before—and for the first time in two weeks, she again felt like that girl who'd sought any excuse to go riding with her good friend Ty and who loved acting with an unblemished passion and delight. Oh, how she'd missed that!

She tested her balance and found that her muscles still remembered how to move and sit despite not having done this in too long. Just like riding a bike, as Ty had told her each first ride after a long break. With her confidence bolstered, she turned her attention back to him and finally asked the question that had been on her mind for two years.

"Last time I was out here, that Christmas Eve under the mistletoe… did you mean to kiss me on the lips?"

Ty eyed her, and for almost a minute, it seemed like he might not answer. At last, he nodded.

As she had feared would happen, a thousand questions rampaged through her mind. Holly, sensing the sudden shift in her mood, sidestepped and snorted nervously, so Shannon slammed the door shut on her thoughts and took a deep breath. She'd be in Northstar for the longest time since before she'd graduated from college, and this time, there were no boyfriends or girlfriends to complicate matters… if the rumor was true and Heather and Ty had broken up just a week ago. The fact that she didn't know if it was true or not made her a terrible friend. She had all the time in the world to figure out what the kiss meant and work with Ty to unravel any potential messes.

When she smiled at him, it came naturally and willingly. "All right, then."

"That's it? You aren't going to ask why?"

"Not today. Right now, I just want to enjoy your company and this magnificent lady and have a good time together like we always do."

"Because you're not ready for any more complications," he surmised.

"Exactly. We have time. More than we've had in years."

"So we do. Fair enough." One side of Ty's lips lifted in a devilish grin. "Of course, I'm hoping it won't *be* a complication."

Another rush of questions followed his statement, but this time, instead of letting them spook her, she laughed. She had no clue what he meant by that, but she knew how she was going to take it until she had the ambition to figure it out—as a reminder that the kiss and whatever had driven Ty to do it could only make their friendship awkward if she let it.

"So, master horseman, how do I ride this gorgeous girl with no bridle?"

* * *

Ty gave Shannon a few brief instructions, then climbed the corral fence to observe her. She was understandably a little rusty, but it didn't take her long to loosen up and trust her muscles to remember what to do, and after that, her natural talent reappeared. Joy soon eradicated the last traces of shyness in her expression, but he couldn't forget he'd seen it. Though he still called her Shy Eyes—a nickname he'd given her very early in their friendship—it had been a long time since she'd been remotely shy around him. A skinny-dipping excursion in the pond on his family's ranch the summer after her sophomore year of college had demolished the last remaining shred of modesty between them. Recalling *that*, Ty lowered his gaze to hide the heat that crawled up his neck and across his face.

Yep, there's that funny tripping thing she makes my heart do.

After her wearied greeting last week, he almost couldn't believe she was here, riding Holly. That she'd brought up the kiss only made this moment more surreal. He'd long been wondering when she was going to ask about it, but that blasé inquiry was *not* what he'd anticipated. Should he be concerned by her unwillingness to dig into his motives? Maybe, but she'd talk about it when she was ready and not a moment sooner, so he needed to be patient. Unfortunately, after two years of waiting for that particular topic to come up and hoping Chris would screw up and give him a chance to explore what he'd uncovered with that impulsive kiss, Ty had little patience left. And watching the graceful, confident movements of Shannon's lithe body and the pleasure that rippled outward from her smile with no one and nothing else to distract him was *not* helping.

On her next pass, he called out to her to stop. She met his request still beaming but with the hint of a frown drawing her brows together, and he instantly regretted interrupting her ride.

"I hate to cut your frolicking short, but Holly already had a pretty good workout before you arrived, and I don't want to push her too hard. She's come a long way and fast, but it's still too early yet to be reminding her of her previous owner."

"I understand. And anyhow, I'll probably be sore enough from *that* little bit," Shannon replied, dropping to the ground. She gave the mare an affectionate pat. "Thanks for the ride, pretty girl."

"Do you have some time to say hi to my family? They've been asking when you might stop by."

"That'd be great. I'd love to see them." She glanced at her watch. "I have almost two hours until I'm supposed to meet Pat and Aeli at the Ramshorn."

"How about you head up to the house? I'll meet you up there after I get Holly taken care of."

"I know you don't need a hand, but would you like one?"

"You know I'm always looking for excuses to spend more time with you, so yeah, I'd love one." He flashed her a grin, and she returned it. *There's my Shy Eyes.*

Ty gave a short, two-note whistle and started toward the barn with Holly following faithfully behind. Shannon walked close beside him with her hand tucked around his arm. If this was a dream and she wasn't really in Northstar, he'd never forgive his imagination for playing such a cruel trick on him. Their frequent phone calls were great, but they were never enough, and their visits—becoming fewer and farther between as the years passed—were always too short. To have a month and a half to reconnect would be a blessing.

Patience, he reminded himself again. "Tell me more about this movie deal. Are you going to make a million bucks on it?"

"Not even close," she laughed. "But if I take it, I'll make more than I've made from the last three plays combined. It's a supporting role, and I'm an unknown in Hollywood, but even so, Macie was able to negotiate a pretty good deal for me."

"It probably helps that Kevin's a good friend."

"That, too. Another reason is how well I can ride a horse, so if I haven't thanked you for being such a great teacher… thank you. That particular skill is what sealed the offer."

"I highly doubt that. You forget that I've seen you on stage and heard you sing. You are incredibly talented, and I guarantee it was that talent alone that brought the offer." He gave her hand a squeeze and shifted his gaze to her face as he spoke again. "That *if* makes me nervous, Shannon. You aren't seriously thinking of turning it down."

There was that guarded look again, the same one she'd worn last Saturday. Almost too softly for him to hear, she said, "Yes, I am."

"Why? Because of that damned tabloid?"

She nodded.

"That's a load of crap, and you're stronger than that. You can't let one piece of garbage stop you from going after your dreams."

"That one piece of garbage was enough to end a three-year-long relationship. What happens if I make it big, Ty? Most likely it won't be just one piece of trash. It'll be a mountain of it, and I don't want to lose anyone else I love over lies, because the people I love are more important to me than some silly dream."

"First of all, it's not a silly dream. Secondly, the people who love you will see right through even the most convincing lie any tabloid writer can come up with."

"Chris didn't."

"Then he didn't really love you, and that is his loss, not yours." With the pain of her breakup now plainly visible in her eyes, Ty stopped walking to hug her close. "Not yours, Shy Eyes."

She sighed raggedly, and when she responded, her voice was muffled by his coat. "I've missed you so much, Ty."

"Hey," he cooed. "We're together again, and we have all the time in the world to enjoy it, right?"

"Right."

From the outside, the Bar E's livestock barn looked just like any other ranch barn in Northstar, but inside, it looked like it might house thoroughbred racehorses rather than quarter horses used for working cattle and sheep and the odd Arabian or pleasure-riding horse. Stalls lined the concrete center aisle, and it was always immaculate, a necessity to draw in the wealthier clientele Ty and his father frequently courted. Training ranch horses paid most of the bills, but it was the pleasure and show horses Ty had convinced his father to include in their repertoire that paid his father's medical bills and had made it possible for them to build the new pavilion. *That* was a blessing, especially on winter days when subzero temperatures made it both agonizing and dangerous to work the horses outside.

Big dreams for the ol' Bar E, Ty's father often joked. And why not? The small ranch had been in their family for four generations, and what could they bring to that legacy if they didn't try to better it?

Shannon, without needing to be told where to find them, fetched the grooming supplies while Ty measured out a ration of oats for Holly, a treat for her hard work today. They talked while they worked, and he was careful to steer their conversation away from troubling topics. Once again, it didn't take long for Shannon to set her worries aside. He'd always admired that about her—her ability to focus on the here and now without letting less pleasant things get in the way. The shadow lingered longer in her eyes, but eventually, it too vanished. A well timed joke about the time they went out riding after a rare cold front dumped four inches of sloppy snow in mid June pushed the last of it away. Ty, riding a horse he'd been working with less than a week, had decided to show off his trick riding skills and had ended up on his ass in a giant, soupy, and frigid puddle. Shannon, laughing so hard she couldn't breathe, had nearly joined him.

"You know, that's the only time I've ever seen you

fall off a horse," she said.

"I wish I could say it *was* the only time, but when I was young and stupid and under the deluded impression that I was invincible, I spent a fair amount of time in the air and on the ground."

"And unlike those few times I've fallen off and you were there to catch me, your dad let you hit the ground."

"Yep. He seemed to think I would be less inclined to be reckless if I knew firsthand how hard the ground is. Unfortunately, he underestimated the allure of the adrenaline rush."

"Thank goodness you outgrew that… after fracturing your wrist and spraining your ankle… how many times?"

"Two for the wrist, four for the ankle, and let's not forget the time I dislocated my shoulder my junior year of college. That's what finally drove Dad's point home. It was my right arm, and damn it was frustrating to not be able to use it."

"As I recalled, your dad didn't let you out of any chores while you were in the sling, either."

"Nope." Ty's face fell, and he ran his hand down Holly's neck one last time before stepping out of her stall and sliding the door closed. "Of course, you can be the most cautious person in the world and still get taken out by the unexpected."

"So very true."

With Shannon's hand again around his arm, they ambled along the boardwalk connecting the barn to his parents' house and then up the steps. Shannon paused to eye the ramp Ty and his brother-in-law had built last fall.

"That's going to take some getting used to," she murmured. "I remember your dad as this big, strong guy with the biggest heart, always laughing and cracking jokes, but now…. I haven't seen him since before the accident. Seeing this makes me feel pretty terrible for not coming out to visit him."

"He's still the same man he always was. You just have to lean down to hug him now." He gave her a reassuring smile. "It wouldn't have changed anything if you'd been out here, and besides, you've been busy."

"That's no excuse. I love your dad, Ty. I should have made time."

Ty shrugged. He'd hoped she would come for a visit to see his father after the freak accident that had left Hunter with a broken back and paralyzed from the waist down, but saying so wouldn't help her feel better nor would it change what had happened. "He's doing great, but I'll never be able to get that image out of my head."

The horse Hunter had been riding had needed to be euthanized. They'd taken an easy trail to one of the many lakes in the Northstar Mountains with the horse's owners as part of the train-the-rider portion of the horse's training, and only moments before the accident, Hunter had suggested he swap horses with the clients' twelve-year-old daughter through the one tricky part of the trail where it skirted the bottom of an old rock slide. The ground along that part of the trail was uneven, so

Hunter figured the girl would be safer on one of the Evanses' experienced horses… and he was right. Out of nowhere, a small boulder broke loose and crashed down the mountain at them in a shower of smaller rocks, spooking the horse, who bucked and stumbled, going down head first on the rocky trail in his panic. The fall broke his neck. Hunter was thrown—or tried to jump clear, Ty still wasn't sure which—and barely missed being crushed by the horse or getting kicked in the head. He'd landed on his back on a log right off the side of the trail, shattering two vertebrae. As terrible as that was, Ty didn't doubt that his father was lucky to be alive.

"I'm sorry, Ty," Shannon whispered, resting her head on his shoulder as they stood on the deck, admiring the craftsmanship of the ramp. "I really am."

"I am, too, but it could have been so much worse. As my dad always says when one of us gets to feeling sorry for him, it could have been Sasha riding Gaston, and she could've died with her horse." His lips twitched, and amusement alleviated some of the despair over his father's injury. "She and her parents come out to visit him every few weeks, which Dad loves, and whenever she's ready to have another horse, I'll be the one to train him. Or her."

"How come you've never mentioned that?"

"Dunno. I guess by the time I could talk about anything but the accident itself and Dad's recovery, it seemed like old news—something I'd already told you."

"Or maybe we're not as close as we used to be

because I'm a terrible friend for letting business get in the way of what matters."

"Maybe so," Ty conceded rather than trying to convince her of a lie, "but the awesome thing about us is that we're such good friends we could probably go for months without talking and pick up right where we left off. However, I'd rather we don't ever put that to the test."

The smile she awarded him was breathtaking. It ignited her green-tinged hazel eyes and was so unrestrained and reassuring. "Me, too."

The front door opened, and Hunter's voice greeted them. "Is that our Shy Eyes I hear?"

"Yes, it is," she replied and left Ty's side to hold the door open for his father.

"I hope you don't expect me to roll out into that cold. Get your backside into the house and get warmed up."

Laughing, Shannon briefly leaned down to hug Hunter, then waved Ty over and followed the patriarch of the Evans family inside. Ty pushed the door closed behind them and hung his coat on a hook on the right wall of the entryway. As always, his parents' house was cozy and filled with the mouth-watering aroma of something cooking. He followed his father and Shannon into the living room, and a commotion erupted as his two nieces and nephew clamored for Shannon's attention while she greeted Ty's mother, brother-in-law, and sister.

"Are you sure you still have a month left?"

Shannon asked April. "You're huge."

"You're telling me," April replied with a hand resting on her very round belly.

"Number four. And since Ty refused to tell me what you're expecting—" Shannon cast a mock scowl over her shoulder at him. "—boy or girl?"

"Boy," April's husband replied. "Which will make us even. No more after this."

"Uh-huh. That's what you said after Rose."

"Danny's got an appointment to get snipped next month," Ty remarked. "Because if he and April have any more kids, there won't be room at the table for mine."

"Whenever you get around to having any," April quipped, "we'll just have to get a bigger table."

"There's an idea," Shannon said. "But that'd be too easy."

Ty ducked into the kitchen while she caught up with his sister and her brood, grabbed a glass out of the cupboard beside the sink, and filled it with the iced tea his mother always kept in the fridge. After being out in the cold for the last several hours, he shouldn't want a cold drink, but it hit the spot. He leaned against the sink sipping his iced tea and enjoying the boisterous conversation in the living room and Shannon's merry laughter as April and Danny's kids poked and prodded and crawled all over her.

"So," his mother said, joining him. "Shannon's back in our lives."

"Mmm-hmm."

"And single, I hear."

"Yep."

"You going to do something about that while she's here?"

"That's the plan."

"Well, get to it. Before some other idiot who isn't good enough for her comes along and yanks her out of your reach again."

Had they not had this exact conversation last Saturday after he'd told her that he and Heather had called it quits and that Shannon was back in Northstar, he might have been shocked. He snorted. No, he wouldn't have, because his outwardly dainty mother had never been one to beat around the bush about… anything. Finesse was Hunter's art, not Phoebe's.

Ty eyed his mother and took a long swallow of his iced tea before responding. "As always, the noon siren in Devyn could teach you a few things about subtlety."

"I've been subtle long enough, Tyler Hunter Evans."

The full name. She's not going to let this go. Lifting a brow, he gave a bark of laughter. "Ha! When have you *ever* been subtle?"

"Fine, if we must split hairs, I've *waited* long enough for you to figure out that you're in love with that girl and have been from the moment you first laid eyes on her." Phoebe curled her hand around his arm much as Shannon had not so long ago. "There's a reason you're such good friends, my boy. You bring out the best in each other."

"Why don't you just come out and say exactly what you're thinking, Mom?" Ty teased. He drained the rest of his tea, rinsed the glass, and set it in the sink. "No point in playing coy now."

"Your father and I want Shannon as our daughter-in-law, Ty. She makes you happy in a way you are only with her."

"And what if she doesn't feel the same? Even if she does, what if she's not ready? She and Chris were together for three years, Mom. That's going to take some time to get over."

"You've never let 'what if' stop you from trying before." She patted his arm and started toward the living room. Turning briefly back to him before she joined the others, she added, "Don't let it stop you now."

Ty didn't follow her into the living room. Instead, he remained leaning against the sink and observed the merry gathering, noting how Shannon interacted with his family as if she were a part of it. She was, just not in the way his mother wanted her to be. Yet.

Phoebe was right. He'd never let the "what if" doubts stop him before—not when he'd entered his first competition as the youngest horse trainer and taken home the blue ribbon, not when Hunter had expressed his concerns about expanding their operation from ranch horses to pleasure and show horses, and not when the accident had forced Ty to take the reins of their business. He wasn't going to let the what ifs stop him now, either.

"Hey, Shy Eyes!" he called. She lifted her head and met his gaze with a vibrant smile. "Would you come here for a minute? Please?"

Nodding, Shannon excused herself and sauntered into the kitchen, and with joy erasing her heartache for the time being, he couldn't take his eyes off her. In moments like this, her shy beauty gleamed brighter than the sun at the height of summer. She tucked her body against his side with an arm wrapped casually around his waist as she gazed into the living room with a faint smile of adoration.

"I didn't realize how much I missed your family. Almost as much as I missed you."

"Believe me. They missed you, too. In fact, my mother finished making that point patently clear only minutes ago."

"Oh? What did she say?"

"Nothing I haven't been considering for a while now."

When he didn't elaborate, she planted herself in front of him with her hands braced on the sink on either side of his waist. Amusement sparkled in her eyes. His heart knocked against his ribs, and he couldn't recall ever being quite so *aware* of her. They'd always been physically relaxed with each other, but this was something quite different.

"Care to clarify for me?" she asked in a voice that was just a little too husky.

"I want to take you on a date. Out to dinner and a

movie or dinner and swimming at the Ramshorn. What-ever you want to do."

She jerked back and gaped. "A date? Like a real, romantic-type, not-as-friends *date*?"

"Yes, a real date."

He searched her expression as she fought to form a response. Her eyes dilated and her cheeks flushed tell-ingly, which kicked his pulse up another gear, but then her brows drew together and sadness dimmed the beau-tiful glow of delight. His heart plummeted. When sadness deepened into agony, it cracked.

"Ty… it's too soon."

"Then we'll go as friends."

That didn't help. Sighing, she turned her gaze out the window behind him, though he doubted she saw an-ything of the sweeping view. He didn't press her, and it was difficult. She'd said it was too soon, but she hadn't said she wasn't interested, and that stirred hope. After more than a minute, she met his gaze again, more com-posed.

"That isn't what you want, though, is it? To stay as friends."

"Of course I want to stay friends. Hence the offer."

"But you want more."

"Yes."

"Which means you think there *is* more."

"I do."

Again, she sighed. "All right. Yes. I admit that I'm curious." Suddenly, her lips parted in a mischievous grin.

"After that kiss, how could I not be?"

Three

TY'S TIGHT WORK SCHEDULE meant the first day he had free for their date was the following Wednesday— the day before Thanksgiving—but Shannon had made a decision to spend time with him, so when she wasn't hanging out with her brother and his family, she was helping Ty work horses. Despite recently breaking up with him, Heather still worked for him, so she was around a lot, too, and Shannon had been certain that would be awkward. Within the first hour on Monday, her worries had been proven unfounded. If she hadn't known Heather and Ty had dated, she never would have guessed it. They were both professionals, and they were also good friends. The initial shock of jealousy that had spawned her concerns faded quickly, but she couldn't forget it, nor could she decide if these odd territorial urges had platonic or romantic origins.

"I can't believe you two shifted back to being friends so quickly," Shannon remarked to the younger woman. They sat together on the fence of the corral, watching Ty as he worked a high-strung Arabian colt with a registered name of Egyptian Shadow Pharaoh on the lunge line. The horse had arrived just last night from Washington, and he was a magnificent animal with a deep black coat that shimmered in the weak winter sunlight.

Heather shrugged. "Wasn't meant to last, and going into it, I knew that. His heart is elsewhere."

"What about *your* heart?" Shannon wasn't brave enough to ask her companion *where* she thought Ty's heart was, and anyhow, she had an idea of what answer Heather would give, which triggered both hope and guilt.

"I'm not the settle-down-and-make-a-family kind, and he is."

"That doesn't exactly answer the question."

"Let me put it this way. I expect there's a guy out there who will make me want those things, but I'm not looking for him yet, and Ty—great as he is—isn't the one, anyhow. I won't be trying to get him back, if that's what you're wondering."

"It really isn't. I was wondering how you're okay with it so fast."

"Well, we *were* together for only a month. I imagine it'd be a different story if it had been three years." The brunette offered a sympathetic smile.

"So, you've been working for Ty for just over a year now, right?"

Heather nodded. "Since shortly after Hunter's accident. All joking and teasing aside, it's been a blessing. Ty's one of the most talented horse trainers I've ever met—even more so than his dad—and this job might end up being my ticket to making my own way without my family's ranch."

Shannon listened as Heather explained that, with two older brothers and a younger sister, there wasn't much left over of the Brown ranch for her, and if she hoped to do more with her life than scrape by, she needed to cut her own path. Shannon had met Heather before, many times, but they'd never had much chance to get to know one another, and despite or perhaps because of their connection through Ty, Shannon was glad to be getting to know her now and enjoyed her tendency to bluntly speak her mind and also her willingness to joke around. It was easy to see why Ty had asked her out, even if it hadn't lasted. She was sharply intelligent and nearly as naturally talented with horses as he was.

As they talked, the sun sank westward and the shadows lengthened, striating the land with glittering golden light and cool blue shadows. Shannon's face was chilled, as were her legs and backside, but she scarcely noticed. The rest of her was warm enough that the discomfort didn't register amidst the beauty of the wintry afternoon and the enjoyable company and work. Shannon had taken Holly out for a ride to the upper pasture earlier in the day, and she'd almost felt as confident in the saddle as she had back in those wonderful summers when she and Ty had ridden every day. Of course, next to him and Heather, she must still look like a novice, but she didn't care. She was having a blast and relaxing.

"What are you two chattering about over here so intently that you didn't hear me say it's quitting time?"

Shannon jumped and barely maintained her perch. She hadn't noticed Ty's approach, but there he was, just feet away astride the big black colt.

"We're gossiping about you," Heather replied while Shannon recovered from her shock. "So bugger off."

"Should I be concerned?"

"No," Shannon answered. "It's all complimentary. Promise."

"Uh-huh. Well, like I said, it's quitting time, so you'll have to save the rest for some other day."

"Mmm. Considering how long he's been waiting for a date with you, I don't think we'll be able to convince him to let us continue our gossip session," Heather mused. "I find it interesting that you two decided to cut a Christmas tree for your first date. It's so domestic, but then again, you already completed the getting-to-know-you stage years ago."

Shannon's jaw dropped at the confirmation of her earlier suspicion of Heather's answer to the unasked question regarding who'd captured Ty's heart. The other woman glanced at her with a brow lifted.

"Don't look so shocked, Shannon. I know you're not so naïve that you haven't already figured out that this is what he's wanted for a while now."

"I…." She snapped her mouth closed. "I haven't thought of it in such exact terms."

Ty cleared his throat.

Heather took the hint and jumped down from the corral fence, rubbing her hands over her thighs to work some warmth back into them. "I don't know about you two, but I'm ready to head inside and get warm. My ass is freezing."

"Guess you've been sitting on it too much today," Ty quipped.

"Well, Shadow here is so new and with Timber out of commission until the farrier can fix that shoe, there isn't exactly a ton for me to do right now, is there, Ty? Aside from gossiping, of course."

"I told you to bring your brother's filly over today."

"I know, but Brock's on my shit list right now for backing over my four-wheeler yesterday, so I'm not inclined to do him any favors."

Ty held his hands up and dropped the topic. "I'm going to take this boy for a walk around the pasture to cool him down. Meet you both in the barn in ten?"

Nodding, Shannon and Heather started toward the barn, jumping right back into their conversation about Ty, horses, Heather's plans for her own business, and Shannon's career as a stage actress. With her decision about the film industry still up in the air, Shannon stayed clear of that vein. They were nearly to the barn when a horse let out a terrified squeal, and they raced up the low hill that separated the barn and corral from the pasture to investigate the source of the commotion.

"Move!" Ty bellowed as Shadow thundered toward them, bucking and leaping.

Shannon and Heather scrambled out of the way, dragging each other along. They stumbled and collapsed in a heap in the snow barely out of the reach of the colt's flying hooves. Ty gripped the Arabian's barrel with his legs and kept his seat despite Shadow's lunging attempts to throw him. His face was a mask of calm focus, and the horse responded to his rider's composure. Ty directed him through the gap between the barn and the corral and back around to the pasture, talking to the black colt in a soft voice. When the horse settled and stopped, quivering, Ty stroked and patted his damp neck.

"You're all right. That little bitty fox can't hurt a big boy like you. Nothing to be afraid of."

Shadow swiveled his ears back to catch Ty's every word, his attention now fully back where it belonged—on his rider.

Shannon watched it all on her butt in the snow, flabbergasted. Ty had maintained his cool through the whole ordeal, and the horse now moved with trusting, ground-eating strides toward the thing that had spooked him.

Shannon took Heather's offered hand up and brushed the snow off herself before turning her attention fully to Ty and Shadow.

As horse and rider neared the clump of leafless willows gathered around the small spring in the middle of the pasture, Shadow's ears flicked toward them, and he tensed, but he continued forward at Ty's urging. A fox bounded out of the thicket, chattering, and this time, Shadow only flinched. Ty held him there through a four-minute standoff until the fox vanished again into the willows. Shadow stretched his neck to sniff, jerking his head back when the fox poked its head out. Ears forward, he appeared to be more curious than afraid. After the fox vanished again, Ty wheeled the colt around and directed him toward the far corner of the pasture.

By the time they returned to the barn, Ty was grinning.

"That was exciting, huh?"

"Yeah, exciting. Sure," Heather retorted. "Not quite the word I would've used. What the hell happened?"

"It appears a fox has decided to make a den by the spring, and something tells me this guy's never seen one before. You two all right?"

"A little colder and wetter but otherwise fine," Shannon replied. "I see what you mean about getting the horse to trust you over his own instincts, and now that my heart has decided it doesn't need to escape my chest, I have to admit that it was pretty amazing how fast you convinced Shadow to trust you. It has to be that innate calmness you exude even when the horse you're riding is trying very hard to buck you off."

"That's exactly it. Horses are smart and sensitive, and they pick up even the tiniest vibrations from you." Ty gave Shadow another pat. "Not bad for a colt who's just barely got the basic commands down. Of course, now we're going to have even less time for our date."

Together, Shannon, Heather, and Ty made quick work of the afternoon chores, and after, Heather headed home, leaving Shannon and Ty alone. She leaned against the doorjamb of the man door of the barn as he double-checked that everything was settled for the night, then stepped out of the way when he pulled the door closed behind them. She couldn't decide if she was actually nervous about their date or only feeling like she should be. Logically, there was no reason to be uneasy; she and Ty had a long, comfortable history, and that hadn't changed simply because they were going on a date with romantic rather than platonic intent.

They tromped with hands held down the boardwalk. His cabin sat on the hill just above the driveway and closer to the barn than his parents' house. Closer to the heart of the ranch, she mused.

"Tell me this shouldn't be weird," she said as they walked.

"This shouldn't be weird."

"Ty, I'm serious."

"So am I. Why should it be? Nothing's changed. We're still best friends, we still work great together, and we still enjoy each other's company, right?"

"Right, but we've opened the door to something else, to a different kind of relationship, and that *does* change things."

"Only if you let it, and then hopefully it'll *add to* our friendship."

"Are you really as confident as you seem, or is it just a show to make me feel better?"

"A little of both, with a heaping side of curiosity and optimism. Maybe I've been told too often by too many people that the key to a strong marriage is marrying your best friend."

Soothed by that sentiment and having seen proof of it in her parents and her brother and sister-in-law, Shannon convinced herself to relax. After all, her nerves probably came from the sudden and unexpected end of her relationship with Chris rather than any genuine doubts about her relationship with Ty—whatever category she chose to place it in. Besides, if she stopped trying to categorize it, she was left with a desire to just *be* with him, to take the joy he brought her and wrap it around herself like a thick fleece blanket on a chilly night.

"I'm overthinking things again, aren't I?"

"Yep."

She shook her head and laughed. "How are you so sure?"

"Because I'm *not* overthinking it. I'm just going with it. Just like I did when I kissed you under the mistletoe."

"Somehow I'm not surprised that wasn't

premeditated."

"It wasn't, but don't think I didn't contemplate it before."

They'd reached the foot of the steps up to the covered deck of his cabin, and she turned abruptly to him with her eyes wide. He didn't react, only continued up the stairs, opened his unlocked front door—how could she forget that no one in Northstar ever locked their doors?—and stepped aside so she could enter first. He strode into the small living room just to the left of the tiny entryway, knelt in front of the wood stove in the corner, and went about stoking the fire without giving any indication that he was going to explain his comment.

Winter sunlight streamed through the big square window that took up much of the front wall of the living room, alighting on the rich golden knotty pine planks of the floor and walls. The cabin was a single-bedroom structure with a tiny kitchen, but it was welcoming, and it suited Ty well. She recalled helping him move into it after he graduated from high school, how excited he'd been to begin carving his own legacy into his family's ranch. Even then, at the age when most kids were anxious to spread their wings and leave the nest, Ty had known exactly what he wanted out of life with a certainty that he would never want to leave Northstar.

She envied him that, especially now when she had no idea what she was going to do with her life. Somehow, despite her successes in college and on the stage, she was still mired in that upheaval of insecure new adulthood.

But Ty had always been like that. Self-assured and confident.

Did that certainty extend to her? Was he already as sure of their path as he was of his career?

Finally, the suspense and curiosity got the best of her. "You've thought about us in romantic terms? For how long?"

"A while. A few times before I kissed you, but a lot more since." He closed the door on the stove and rose to his feet. "You can't tell me you've never once wondered if there might be more than simple friendship."

"Sure I did. We met when we were teenagers, right at the height of hormonal curiosity about the opposite sex. But you had a girlfriend, and then we got to be friends, and I forgot about it."

"Forgot about it or ignored it?"

"A little of both, I suppose."

"So it crossed your mind at the beginning, which means it might be safe to say that it was the circumstances rather than a lack of romantic attraction that relegated us to the wonderful but not-enough friend zone?"

"I—" She clamped her mouth closed when his eyes lit up with a smug gleam. Folding her arms, she pressed her lips into a flat line and raised her brows at him. "That was a sneaky trick, Tyler Evans."

"At least you didn't use the middle name," he muttered. "It *was* sneaky. I'm sorry. Shall we go get that Christmas tree? Saw's already with the sled."

He still hadn't answered her question, but even as

curious as she was to know how long he'd been hoping for a deeper relationship with her, she had neither the courage to press him for the answer nor the desire to further delay their date. As it was, they had maybe an hour of sunlight left.

Is this even a real date?

Other than the fact that they'd said it was, it didn't feel like one. It felt like two friends going out to play in the snow like they had many times before when she and her parents had come out to spend the holidays with her brother and his family. Maybe it'd feel more real after they'd found, cut, and hauled the tree back to his house and headed up to the Ramshorn for dinner.

And maybe I'm still overthinking it.

She followed him out to the shed beside his cabin and waited while he pulled his snowmobile out and attached the matching sled behind it. Then he straddled the machine and patted the seat behind him, inviting her to sit. Again, this wasn't anything they hadn't done before, but when she tucked her knees in behind his, wrapped her arms around his waist, and laid her cheek briefly against his back, she noticed something new. This being officially designated as a date, she was free to enjoy the feel of their bodies pressed together without needing to keep other urges quiet by reminding herself that they were *friends*.

Ty drove the snowmobile along the ranch road at a leisurely pace toward the eastern edge of the upper pasture, stopping only to open and close gates. They didn't talk; the growl of the snowmobile's engine prevented much discussion and they were content to enjoy the simplicity of each other's company. When they reached their destination, Ty shut the snowmobile down, climbed off, and offered a hand to Shannon.

"Where shall we start looking?" he inquired, grabbing the handsaw from a shallow compartment built beneath the deck of the sled. He dropped a coil of rope on the seat of the snowmobile and came to stand beside Shannon to eye the younger trees at the edge of the stand of evergreens.

"That little one right there—see it? It's about five feet tall—is just about perfect for the space you have. It's narrower than the rest, so it won't take up your entire living room."

He tilted his head and studied the tree in question for a moment, then he offered her a lop-sided grin. "If it wasn't such a perfect tree, I might think you were trying to put a quick end to our date."

"I'm just that good at picking Christmas trees… and that anxious to head to the Ramshorn for a nice long soak in hot water. It's not exactly tropical out here, and we've been outside most of the day. And I'm hungry."

Chuckling, he trudged over to the tree with saw in hand and started sawing. She wrapped her gloved hands around the trunk toward the top, grateful for the thick material that saved her skin from the sharp needles. The spicy fragrance of the spruce's sap and wood filled the air with Christmas cheer as Ty cut, and Shannon inhaled deeply while she held the tree steady, wondering if he and his family still practiced the tradition of planting new saplings to replace the trees they harvested. She hoped so. She wondered, too, if this was one they'd planted. Since they usually took their trees from this stand, it was quite possible.

"It might be," Ty replied when she asked. He sawed through the trunk, and Shannon lifted the tree out of the way. He hesitated, staring at the stump with a frown of concentration and his lips moving ever so slightly. It took her a moment to figure out that he was counting the tree's rings. "I couldn't honestly say. I'd've been too young to remember this one. It's about twenty-five years old."

"It's that old?" She peered at the stump, noting how close together the rings were. "Why do you suppose it's so small?"

"It's at the edge of the stand, so it's too far from the spring, and this south-facing slope isn't an ideal spot for evergreens. The snow melts off too fast and just runs down the hill."

"There's a spring here, too?"

He nodded. "It's not much of one, though. Barely enough to make the ground a little soggy."

"Huh."

Either of them could have carried the tree alone, but they did it together, using the rope to secure it on the sled with the trunk toward the snowmobile. Then, rather than head immediately back to Ty's, they sat on the seat with their legs facing west to watch the sun's light turn the snow to a glittering golden blanket. The contrasting shadows deepened into indigo, and the setting was nothing short of magical. Ty draped his arm around her shoulders, and she leaned into him, warmed by more than the faint body heat that escaped his heavy winter clothing. For once, she didn't try to analyze the situation and simply enjoyed the incredible beauty before her as the sun sank behind the western ridges and soon after ignited the scattering of gauzy clouds with molten gold.

This right here—the failing day with its stunning show of blue and gold and white and the untainted peace and holiday festiveness that curled around her as cozily as Ty's arms—was perfect. Smiling, she exhaled and watched the cloud of her breath drift away.

"So… how long have you been thinking about taking me on a date?" she asked. "Since you didn't answer me earlier."

"Pretty much from the beginning, but until I kissed you, it was little more than idle curiosity."

"And after?"

"I think you know the answer to that already."

She did. That brief taste had apparently fanned the flames of idle curiosity into a desire for more rather than doused them.

"Why did you lie to Chris about it?"

"At the time, he made you happy. I couldn't ruin that for you." He rested his cheek on the top of her head.

"Kissing you was stupid and impulsive, but I don't regret doing it. Selfishly, I don't, but I *am* sorry that it's hurt you."

"Other than Chris using it against me, it hasn't, and that wasn't your fault." Because she didn't like it when he was in pain—and he was, if the catch in his voice was anything to go by—any more than he liked it when she was, she tilted her face up to him and grinned. "Besides, you're an even better kisser than I thought you'd be."

He laughed softly and caressed her chilled cheek with his thumb. The rough material of his glove against her skin elicited a shiver from her, but she imagined it was nothing compared to what skin against skin would do. That thought, added to the gratitude that accompanied the news that he had already put her happiness before his own desire, convinced her that there was indeed potential between them. A lot of it.

"Since we're on a date, does that mean I get another taste?"

The smile he afforded her was disarmingly tender. "Not yet. You've had a rough few weeks, and I want to ease you into this as best I can. As you've said, we have a bit of time to see what happens."

She didn't say it out loud, but right then, she needed and was ready to embrace what he offered. It didn't matter where that light of adoration shining in his eyes came from; it was enough to know that she was loved.

"All right, let's go get this tree set up and get the

lights on it," she sighed, grudgingly giving in to the inevitable end of this flawless moment. "We can discuss the details of our second date while we're at it."

"Our second date?"

"Mmm-hmm. I think we should go shopping in Butte for Christmas presents and decorations. I don't have many of the former, and you said you don't have any of the latter." She grinned and stretched her neck to kiss his cheek. "Then we can come home and finish decorating together."

"Sounds wonderful. When?"

"Are you feeling up to braving the Black Friday madness?"

"For you, anything."

Unexpectedly, he stole a quick kiss. It was just a peck, a fleeting brush of his lips against hers, but it was more than enough to leave her wanting more.

"I think some mistletoe should be at the top of that list," she murmured, suddenly wanting very much to reenact that first kiss and see if it was as exciting as she remembered.

Ty chuckled.

* * *

Two days ago on their Christmas-tree-cutting expedition with her cheeks made rosy by the cold and her eyes softened by contentment as they'd sat together to watch the sun go down, Shannon had been gorgeous, but now as she sat in the middle of his living room floor surrounded by newly purchased cartons of fragile glass ornaments and draped in shimmery tinsel garland, she was adorable and ever more irresistible. They'd arrived back from Butte less than an hour ago after a two-hour drive over slick, snowy roads, but it hadn't been long enough for him to forget how cheerful and unperturbed by the crush of stressed Black Friday bargain hunters she'd been. As much time as she spent in the city, even throngs of holiday shoppers in Montana must seem like an ordinary crowd, but it amused him nonetheless.

He set the two mugs of steaming apple cider on the coffee table within reach and joined her on the floor to help untangle the ornament hangers.

"I still can't believe you didn't have *anything* but lights," she muttered, frowning as she worked a few slender hangers loose with her nimble fingers.

"Lights I borrowed from my parents just for you." He laughed softly. "Why is that so surprising? I don't spend much time here, and I don't have a roommate to help me decorate and celebrate like you do. Besides, there's always plenty of Christmas spirit at my parents' and at April and Danny's to give me my holiday fix."

"So?"

"So there's not much point in decorating my house when it's just me here alone, is there?"

"But it's Christmas. And what about your girlfriends? Didn't they ever inspire you to decorate?"

"Nope. Only you, Shy Eyes." He tucked an arm around her shoulder and pulled her close. "You're cute."

She hung a loop of the garland around his neck and

pressed her lips to his cheek. "So are you, Mr. Practical."

"I suppose that's a nice way to say it. Better than Mr. Too Busy or Mr. Lazybones, either of which is probably more accurate."

Shannon took a sip of her cider, then bounced to her feet and piled the rest of the garland in his lap before getting to work hanging ornaments. He stretched his legs out in front of him with his hands braced behind him and observed her for a few minutes. Clad in a sinfully soft powder blue sweater and faded blue jeans with her feet snuggled in warm, fuzzy socks that matched her sweater in color and her rich, dark auburn hair falling loose down her back, she brought him far more seasonal spirit than either the refreshingly fragrant tree or the Christmas songs playing on the radio. Tilting his head, he listened for a moment to a Country version of "I'll be home for Christmas." It was a fitting song, he mused with his lips curving in appreciation.

This was a thousand times better than sitting alone in his undecorated cabin, and he cherished every moment of it, but he couldn't help but wonder again if it was too good to be true. He was more than a little dumbfounded at how quickly and comfortably Shannon had slipped into this new chapter of their relationship. The line between friendship and romance was, at the moment, so blurred that he couldn't be sure which side they stood on. She didn't seem to have any concerns about him hugging her or kissing her—though they hadn't tried the latter again since the other day—but they'd always been comfortable with each other. For God's sake, they'd seen each other naked years ago.

I'm not going to worry about it, he vowed. *I'm going to enjoy crossing the line and hope we stay on this side of it.*

The woman centered so firmly in his thoughts glanced over his shoulder and caught him watching. "Mr. Lazybones indeed. Get your butt up off that floor and help me."

"Yes, ma'am."

Pushing off the floor, he grabbed another box of ornaments. It was amazing how even the clear mini lights they'd wrapped around the tree the day before yesterday and the few ornaments she'd already hung made the little spruce look like a real Christmas tree instead of nothing more than a piece of the outdoors he'd brought inside.

"Are you still up for helping me put up lights on the deck when we're done with this?" he asked.

"Absolutely. I don't have anywhere else to be this evening. Pat and Aeli both have to work, and the kids are hanging out with the Conners."

"In that case, I'd like to treat you to some elk stew as thanks for your assistance."

"Mmm, elk stew. That sounds delicious. Count me in."

They got more serious about decorating, and as they worked, Shannon sang along with the radio. At the moment, it was an instrumental version of "Carol of the Bells," but she sang the words. Ty hadn't forgotten how beautiful and clear her voice was, exactly, but hearing it was something different from remembering it. It was amazing how versatile her voice was, how she could soften it or sharpen it at will, and the purity of it…. It was as if her voice was her soul, and when she sang, that spirit was on display for everyone to hear and feel. How could Chris have heard her sing and still believe she was capable of the deceit he'd accused her of?

When she caught him staring at her, her expression turned shy, but she didn't stop singing. An image of her singing their kids to sleep with that voice sprang into his mind, so clear and so sweet in its intensity that he felt like he'd been kicked in the chest by a horse. He couldn't breathe. To cover, he stepped over to the table to take a drink of his cooling apple cider.

Where in the hell did that *come from?*

He hadn't a clue, but he couldn't get it out of his head.

"Ty? What's wrong?"

"Nothing." He offered her a smile. "After all these years, I'm still in awe of your voice. Any more news on the possible record deal?"

"Some. Kevin's friend is definitely interested, but Kevin is dragging his feet setting up a meeting. I think he wants to make sure I sign the contract for the movie first." She snorted. "If there's any *quid pro quo* happening between Kevin and me, it's that. He wants me in his movie, so he's dangling the record talks in front of me like a carrot on a stick."

"Except that you want the movie deal, too, don't

you?"

"It would be a blast, I'm sure, and it would be a pretty big thing to add to my résumé, but honestly, it's the music industry I want to break into, not Hollywood."

"But if you could do both, you'd want to, right?"

"Sure. I've always been fascinated by how movies are made, and I'd love to be a part of it."

She talked about it like it was nothing out of the ordinary, like he might talk about mucking out stalls or mending fences—as nothing more than any routine part of any job. How could he be anything but besotted with her? *No point in denying that I am.*

"Why are you looking at me like that?" she asked, her eyes widening when she caught his appraisal.

"You have no idea how incredibly talented you are. I'd bet you don't have a clue in that pretty head of yours why Kevin wants you in his movie so badly. You are amazing, Shy Eyes. All the more so because you *don't* realize it."

She lowered her eyes, and while a faint smile danced over her features, it wasn't one of pride or vanity but of humility. After all these years of hearing similar statements from him and her family and everyone around her, she was still uncomfortable with such blatant praise. She might not be the most exotic beauty in any room, but she definitely had the power to take a man's breath away and make him dream of claiming her in every way— friend, lover, partner... wife. For over nine years, he'd counted himself blessed to call her the first, but the inkling of a desire for the others hadn't dawned on him fully until he'd kissed her.

Glancing around his littered floor, he located the tree topper she'd picked out—a rustic country angel with red-brown yarn for hair, red and white gingham ribbon around her waist, and a dress of burlap stamped with glittery red snowflakes. He picked up mistletoe and hooked it in the hands of the angel before settling her in her place at the top of the tree. Then he turned to Shannon, twined their fingers together, and tugged her close. Slipping his fingertips teasingly under her chin, he inclined his head toward the angel with her mistletoe bouquet, and when Shannon's lips curved with understanding, he kissed her tenderly. When she submitted, he deepened the kiss, asking for a little more but determined to keep it from surpassing their first kiss.

"Been wanting to do that again for two years," he murmured. "Did it live up to the memory?"

"Better," she purred. "Because now I get to do what I wanted to then… only this time, I have nothing to feel guilty about."

She didn't give his muddled brain a chance to decipher what she meant, threading her arms around his neck with her body pressed enticingly against his and her mouth demanding more than what he'd offered a moment ago.

She tasted of apples and cinnamon and warmth, and he answered her demand with his own. He rocked his hips toward her as she opened her mouth to permit his tongue entrance. She kissed like no one he'd ever been with—shy and confident at once, a combination that should be impossible. So much for not outdoing that first kiss.

Aware that he was on the verge of losing his head, he grudgingly released her mouth but couldn't resist stroking his thumb over her silky cheek. Her eyes were still closed, and he almost begged her to open them, but she was so exquisite with her lashes resting against her cheeks and her mouth open slightly as if she was lost in his touch and unwilling to find her way out. He hoped that was the case.

"We don't have a lot of daylight left," he whispered, "so if the tree is done to your satisfaction, we should probably turn our attention to the outdoor decorations."

Her eyes sprang open, and for the moment before her brain came back online, her pupils were so dilated that the irises were slim rings around bottomless black wells, more green than hazel. Or maybe they were just picking up the color of the tree. Either way, the blatant desire in her eyes was a punch to the gut, and he choked back a groan. To soften the abrupt end of what had been an exquisite moment for them both, he touched his lips to hers once more, then stepped away to gather the boxes of lights she'd picked out for his deck.

After they shrugged into their coats and gloves, Ty settled his favorite black cowboy hat on his head and followed Shannon out into the brisk November afternoon.

While she was preoccupied with the bigger, older-style colored lights like his parents usually put around their roofline, he stretched and untangled a string of clear mini lights. He hadn't wanted anything too fancy, just a few lights to make the place look a little more festive, but he hadn't told her that, curious to see what she would choose with his tastes in mind. She'd picked exactly what he would have himself, and that was both surprising and not. Their longstanding friendship meant she knew him as well as his parents and sister, but either she'd sidelined her own preferences or hers matched his. He suspected the latter, and that's what surprised him. The Shannon he'd first met and become friends with would have undoubtedly preferred the simple decorations he liked, but she'd spent a number of years in the limelight with the influences of urbanite sophistication all around her. Shouldn't that have left a mark on her?

That it apparently hadn't spoke of an innate strength and sincerity he found very appealing. Wanting to see her grinning again like a young girl untroubled by thoughts of broken relationships and monumental business decisions, he wrapped himself in a string of lights, then connected it to the extension cord already plugged in to the outlet and leaned against post of the deck's roof. "What do you think? Should I apply for a job to be a holiday decoration?"

"I imagine there are a number of women who would pay good money to have you decorating their front door. You're the perfect combination of sexy and adorable." She laughed heartily. "I can see the ad now. 'Reserve a Christmas Cowboy today. Comes complete with your very own light-up cowboy.' I don't think all those horses will train themselves, though, so you probably shouldn't quit your day job. There are a lot of guys who are decorative but not many who can do what you do."

Did she just call him sexy? Ty ignored it. There was no way he was going to dwell on that just yet. "Speaking of horses, what do you say to inviting Ant and Iris horseback riding? Seth may be too young yet to be out in this cold."

"I'm sure they'd love that. And maybe we could bring Hunter and Emma, too."

"I'll ask if April wouldn't mind letting Seth hang out with Rose so neither of them are left out."

"Did we just set another date?"

"I think we did. How's this Wednesday right after school sound? I don't think Pat and Aeli work that night, and they might appreciate a date night, too."

"I'll bet they would." She tilted her head and studied him with her eyes narrowed, then shook her head and smiled.

"What? Did I suddenly sprout a second nose?"

"That's not it." She laughed lightly, but then she sighed. "I forget sometimes how considerate you are. I mean, I *know* you are, but I don't always remember to appreciate it."

"Wasn't Chris considerate?"

She shook her head. Whether she was answering with a negative or trying to convey that it was something she didn't feel like talking about, he had no idea. So he probed deeper.

"Go ahead and compare us, Shy Eyes. I'm secure in who I am."

"I know you are, but no."

"Why not? We've both held the same position in your life now, so it's probably pretty natural to compare us."

Again, she shook her head, and he didn't like the sadness that shadowed her eyes. "I don't want to compare you. You're two different men, and…. I just don't want to do it, all right?"

"I'm sorry I brought it up," he murmured. "That was thoughtless of me."

"Believe me, Ty. You aren't the thoughtless one."

Later, when all the decorations had been put up and Shannon deemed his house adequately trimmed for Christmas, they sat on the couch together with bowls of the hearty elk stew he'd had simmering in the Crockpot to watch the setting sun color the landscape out the big window first in fiery reds, oranges, yellows, and pinks and then in pastel gold, peach, blue, and lavender. That anguish had vanished from Shannon's gaze, but Ty remembered it and tucked his arm around her. The way that sadness appeared and disappeared told him a lot about her state of mind, and he hoped she wasn't simply trying to pretend she was okay moving on with him if she wasn't.

The last thing he wanted to be was a rebound. He cared too much about Shannon to settle for meaning so little to her.

Four

"AUNT SHANNON, WHAT ARE you doing here?"

She took the coat belonging to the little boy who looked so like her brother off its peg in the arctic entry of the rural schoolhouse and held it out to him. "Didn't your mom and dad tell you I was picking you up today?"

"Uh…."

"Yeah, they did, Ant," the boy's blonde-haired, green-eyed sister piped, stuffing her arms into the coat Shannon now held out for her. "They told us last night, 'member?"

"I guess. Oh! You're taking us horseback riding with Ty Evans, right?"

"That's right, and we don't have a ton of time to get up to the Bar E if we want more than a few minutes of daylight to ride, so let me just go talk to Mrs. Fitzwater for a second, and then we'll head up."

"Hunter and Emma are coming, too, aren't they?" Ant asked.

"Yes, but they're riding home with their mom."

"What about Seth?" Iris asked. "Are he and Rose coming, too?"

"No, it's a bit chilly out, but they're going to play together at the Evanses' while we ride. Seth's already down at their house." Shannon excused herself from her niece and nephew for a minute to track down their teacher. Ty's sister was currently helping one of her other students clean up a spill. "Hey, April, we're heading up to the ranch. Anything I need to pass on to Pat and Aeli about homework before we go?"

April glanced up from her task. "No homework for Iris, but Ant has some math to finish. See you out there in a bit."

Shannon nodded. "See you in a little while," she added to April's eldest children, Hunter and Emma, who were the same ages as Ant and Iris—eight and five-and-a-half.

"Yeah, we can't wait!" Emma said. "Thanks, Shannon."

She nodded acknowledgement to the little girl and headed back into the arctic entry to herd her nephew and niece outside into the chilly afternoon. Her brother and sister-in-law had sent their children to school more bundled up than usual in preparation for their afternoon ride, and they looked like a pair of brightly colored marshmallows—Antony in bright red and navy blue and Iris in "not too girly" ice blue and purple.

"Ty's new horse's name is Holly, isn't it?" Iris asked.

"Yes, it is."

"That's neat. I'm gonna ride a Christmassy-named horse on a Christmas trail ride."

"If he lets you ride her," Ant retorted.

Shannon smiled indulgently as they launched into a debate about which horse they'd each ride, and she realized that they'd spent a fair amount of time on the Bar E... and the Lazy H, C-Diamond, and Royal R Ranches, by the sound of it. Of course they had. This was Northstar where everyone knew everyone else and neighbors were as close as family.

Have I been away so long that I've forgotten that? Apparently so, if she was shocked by their stories about other wintertime rides with Will and Jessie Hammond. And here she'd thought she was doing something special for them and that Ty was the most considerate man she'd ever dated. Well, that last part was true. Even if he'd made the same offer to Ant and Iris before, it didn't lessen the gesture. He'd thoughtfully provided her the excuse and the means to spend time with her niece and nephew without having to give up time with him. And time with him was something she dearly wanted and needed right now. She still had her moments of anger and angst over Chris's words, but the soothing balm of Ty's patience and unassuming nature dulled the sting significantly.

"Um, Aunt Shannon? Isn't that the driveway to the Bar E?" Ant asked.

She'd nearly driven passed it and now had to pump her brakes to keep her SUV from sliding on the icy main road. "Sorry, guys."

"What were you thinking about?" Iris inquired.

"Things I probably shouldn't be… and a few I should."

"Were you thinking about Chris?"

"Yeah, I was."

"Dad says he was mean to you and that he made you sad so you won't be kissing him anymore."

Shannon couldn't help but smile at Iris's innocent way of putting it. "Yes, he was, and no, I won't be kissing him anymore."

"What about Ty? Do you want to kiss him?"

Insightful little thing, Shannon mused. "We'll see."

"I like Ty better than Chris, anyhow."

"Me, too," Ant agreed. "He's a lot nicer."

Shannon whimpered a little, feeling like an invisible hand had taken hold of her heart and squeezed. This was *not* what she wanted to be discussing with her brother's too-smart-for-their-own-good children on their fun outing. After what he'd said to her, Chris didn't deserve to have the power to sour her day. Admittedly, pushing him from her mind was a form of hiding when what she needed to do was face the fact that what she'd thought was love was only a lie, but she wasn't quite ready to sit down and analyze her failed relationship with Chris just yet. At the same time, she was uncomfortably conscious that she was doing a disservice to Ty and whatever chance they had as a couple.

That sounds so weird. She wrinkled her nose and parked her SUV in front of the barn and shut the engine off. *And yet… strangely right.*

He must've heard her pull up because he strode out of the barn with a saddle dangling from his hand and waved. Without waiting for her to excuse them, Ant and Iris burst out of the car with an enthusiastic greeting for Ty, who hitched the heavy saddle over his shoulder to give them each a one-armed hug.

"Ty, can I ride Holly? Can I *please?*" Iris begged.

"You bet, kiddo."

"Can I ride that new horse Aunt Shannon told me about? Shadow?"

"Sorry, Ant, but he's not nearly ready for any but a very experienced hand. How 'bout I give you Trigger?"

"Which one's Trigger?"

"The big black quarter horse I'm training for the Ramshorn."

"Oh, right! I remember him. He's the one Luke rode this summer on that trail ride we all went on up to Sawtooth."

"That's right."

April showed up with her kids in tow a few minutes later, and Ty refused to let her help saddle horses. With a hug and a kiss on his cheek, she gleefully obeyed his admonishment to go rest and hurried up to their parents' house. Both Ant and Hunter were surprisingly skilled at saddling horses, so the work went quicker than Shannon had figured. The boys would each get their own horse while the girls would ride Holly together, taking turns with the reins. Shannon helped the kids onto their horses while Ty ducked into the barn again.

When he came back out with bright red and green ribbons festooned with bright brass jingle bells, she stared and watched as he affixed a set to the breast collar of each saddle.

"Jingle bells?" she inquired, brows lifted.

He shrugged. "Who says I'm not a festive guy? Besides, it's serving a dual purpose."

"Oh? What's the reason other than making a bunch of kids smile?"

"Teaching Shadow to accept odd noises."

Holly, Trigger, a gray gelding aptly named Snowcloud, and Marquessa, the bay mare Shannon would be riding, couldn't care less about the bells, and she wondered if Ty had already introduced the horses to them. Shadow, on the other hand, eyed the bells with his ears forward, curious. He showed no sign of distress, however, when Ty jingled them behind the Arabian's head, near his hooves, and under his belly. When he attached them to the colt's breast collar, Shadow only sniffed them with mild interest.

"Do you use bells often in training?" she asked.

"Not too often, but yeah. It makes it harder for the

horse to hear other things, and while some might say I'm making it up, I've found it assists in the process of teaching them to trust me for the very reason that one of their key senses is distorted."

"That makes sense, I guess."

"All right, is everyone ready for this?"

"Yeah!" all four kids cheered at once.

Shannon climbed into Marquessa's saddle, and Ty—showing off a bit for their nieces and nephews—slapped Shadow's rump and executed a perfect flying mount, using the horse's momentum to pull him into the saddle. With bells jingling magically and the horses' legs swishing the powdery snow that'd fallen over the last couple days, they set off on the ranch driveway toward the main road through the Northstar Valley. The plan was to ride up to the Bedspread so they could show off their riding skills to Pat and Aelissm and then loop down through the subdivision where Shannon's rental cabin was located to Clark Creek Road, and take the Sheep Field trail to the access road that connected the Bar E's pastures. It'd be twilight before they finished their ride, and rumor had it that the Evanses would have dinner and hot chocolate waiting for them after they unsaddled the horses.

They alternately sang Christmas carols and quizzed Ty about training horses as they rode along the groomed snowmobile trail that ran beside the main road. Their stop at the Bedspread Inn was a short one, barely long enough to let Pat and Aeli know that Ant had math homework, and then they were off down Elkhorn Road. Betty Burns was just closing up her store when they trotted past, and she waved.

Shannon's cheeks ached equally from the cold and smiling so much. Ty was a generous and amicable host, and he had their younger companions laughing uproariously with jokes. She watched him, noting how riding was as natural to him as walking and trying hard not to pay too much attention to how good he was with the kids. He was going to make a great father some day, and she had to ignore the prickle of envy that came with pondering what lucky woman would catch his eye. The evidence of the past couple weeks pointed to her being that woman, and there was certainly a lot about him that appealed to her. There always had been. But she was alarmingly aware of how recently she'd been dating another man and of how difficult it was to discern the difference between her friendship with Ty and this new romantic exploration. What if she was latching on to Ty only because she'd been hurt and was hungry for any kind word or gesture? That would mean Ty was nothing more than a rebound. And she couldn't let him be. Such a situation would damage her friendship with him, possibly beyond repair.

"You're gonna give yourself a headache thinking so hard."

She jerked her head up to find him riding directly beside her with a concerned frown shadowing his handsome face. When her horse hopped a little, she took a deep breath to ease her shock. "Sorry."

"Don't know why, but you'll miss the best part of the ride if you're too lost in thought to see it."

At once, she realized they'd ridden all the way to the aspen grove on the trail down to the Sheep Field. It was here her brother had married Aelissm in that simple but incredible autumn ceremony. She couldn't remember crossing the creek, but obviously they had and were now at the crest of the hill overlooking the Sheep Field. And the sun had lit the sky on fire. She inhaled sharply as she took in the spectacular contrast of vivid yellow, orange, and pink clouds against the glowing blue of the sky and noted how the reflected light brushed the snowy landscape with a rosy tint.

"Oh, wow," she breathed.

They sat silently on their horses beneath the bare branches of the aspen grove until the sunset faded into dim purple, each and every one of them in the thrall of the spectacle.

Ty broke the spell when he addressed Ant and Iris. "Do you two know that this is where your parents got married?"

They nodded vigorously.

"Mom was so beautiful," Ant said.

"And Dad was so handsome," Iris added. "We've seen the pictures. It was magical. Just like tonight."

Shannon agreed on both counts. This evening came straight out of a cowboy Christmas fairytale with the glittering snow and merry jingling of the bells. Again, it was brought to her attention that Ty was as patient and attentive with kids as he was with horses. This time, though, she didn't try to ignore it. She let it wash through her and soothe her worries. Even if they ended up deciding that the desire that had driven Ty to kiss her that first time wasn't enough to last, she was wrong to think their friendship would suffer. It was too strong, and Ty would fight to save it. So would she.

They headed back to the ranch as the sky darkened, unsaddled the horses, and arrived at Hunter and Phoebe's house just as dinner came out of the oven—a spaghetti-inspired casserole Ty's mother called Italian sausage rigatoni that was a favorite of all six kids.

When it was time to take Ant, Iris, and Seth home, Shannon didn't want to go. Ty offered to help her get her brother's kids settled in the SUV, and after they were secure in their seatbelts, she lingered outside with him.

"So… Heather was right," she said quietly, giving voice to the observation that had been nagging her all evening. "You're serious about wanting to settle down."

"Yeah, I am. Not that I ever partied it up or felt the need to sow my wild oats, as they say, but I'm almost twenty-seven. It's time."

"Well, I can tell you one thing. You're going to be a great father. Seriously, Ty. You are wonderful with kids."

"Thanks." His lips quirked into a lopsided smile. "Must be all the time I spend with my sister's kids. I've had lots of practice. But the thing I've found is that, if you spend enough time around the little buggers, you start wanting some of your own."

Shannon nodded in agreement. Whenever she got to play with her niece and nephews, that maternal clock started ticking louder.

"I'm kinda hoping you might be the one to help me out with that."

For the second time tonight, he caught her unaware. She snapped her head back and stared at him, but shock quickly gave way to something else. Was he *that* certain about them? How could he be when she couldn't even decide if they were even a couple yet? Technically, yes, she supposed they were, but were they *actually*, in every sense of the word?

"I should get these three home to their parents," she murmured.

"I'm sorry. I shouldn't have said that. I was out of line." He let out a breath. "Again."

"It's okay. I'm just adjusting still, I guess." She almost said that the idea of settling down with him was appealing, but she didn't dare. "Don't take my reaction to mean that I'm against the idea, Ty. I don't know what I am yet."

"Understandable. And I'm probably not helping you figure it out by being pushy. I just feel like I've been waiting for this for a long time."

"You're not being pushy. Straightforward, yes, but not pushy."

He held out his arms, and she didn't hesitate before walking into them. She tucked hers around his waist and let him hold her, sighing and wishing she could close the door firmly and permanently on Chris, but it was too fresh and the desire for resolution too strong.

"I know you need to get the kids home," Ty said gently, "but before you do, I wanted to invite them and you to a cookie-baking party on Friday."

"A cookie-baking party?"

"Yep. April, Danny, their kids, our folks, and I are baking cookies for the potluck on Saturday, and we're all hoping you four will come down to help."

"Sounds like a blast. I'm supposed to be watching them Friday evening, anyhow, so that'd be perfect."

"It's another date, then."

"Yes, it is, but I'd like the one after to be just you and me again."

"Mmm, I would, too, but that's unlikely."

"Oh? What else to you have in mind?"

"The potluck. Everyone's going to be there to watch the Bobcats' play in the semi-finals."

"That's right! I can't believe I forgot. Okay, so the date after that."

He grinned. "Getting a little ahead of yourself, aren't you?" How 'bout we see how these next two dates go before we start planning the next one."

"Says the guy who said not two minutes ago that he wants me to be the mother of his children."

"Still do. But you can't jump straight to the finish line, right? You have to take it one step at a time."

She didn't respond. Instead, she rose up on her

toes and kissed him. For as brief a touch as it was, it set her heart to humming. "Or two. See you Friday… and Saturday."

"Not tomorrow?"

"I told Pat and Aeli I'd help out at the Bedspread, but I'll try to stop by after."

"I'll keep an eye out for you. G'night, Shy Eyes."

"Good night, Ty…ger."

He tipped his head back and laughed. "Been a long time since you've called me that."

"I may have to reintroduce it to my vocabulary."

He stole another quick kiss, then stepped back to watch her drive away.

After she dropped Ant, Iris, and Seth off at their parents', Shannon headed home to find a message on her answering machine. She pressed play and smiled when she heard her roommate's voice on the other line.

"Hey, chica, hope you're still having a great time in Northstar. Kinda wishing Marc and I were there with you. But that's not why I called. Chris stopped by a few minutes ago looking for you. I told him you were visiting your brother. I hope I didn't screw up by telling him that, but he sounded really sad. I think he might've realized that he screwed up big time. Anyhow, call me back when you can."

Shannon grabbed the cordless and flopped on the couch but didn't immediately call Celeste. After her wonderful evening with Ty, the reminder of Chris was an unwelcome intrusion. It was almost fifteen minutes before she worked up the motivation to call her roommate back, and when Celeste mentioned a belief that Chris might be looking to make up with her, she shifted the conversation away from him. She didn't want to talk about her ex. She'd much rather talk about Ty.

* * *

"This is a lovely picture," Phoebe remarked to her son when he ventured into the kitchen to pull the next batch of cookies out of the oven. "Only one thing that'd make it even lovelier. Do you know what that is?"

"I have a guess," Ty replied, "but I'm sure you're going to explain it to me anyhow."

He arranged the cookies on a rack to cool.

"If those kids in there with Shannon were yours and hers rather than her brother's, *that* would make this picture perfect." She eyed him pointedly. "I want grand-babies."

"You have three already, and in a month or so, you'll have a fourth."

"And so far, not one of them is showing the same talent for working with horses that you and your father have. I want to know that everything you two have built here will continue."

"Emma's already pretty good with the horses, and Hunter's not too bad, either."

"Yes, she is, but she doesn't have the gift."

"Mom, she's five. Give her time, and I'll bet she picks it up."

"We knew you had it when you were still in diapers,

Ty. It's not something you can learn. It's something that comes from the very core of your soul."

"The way the world's going, there may not be a need for our services by the time any kids I have are old enough to take over from me."

"I highly doubt that. Horses are too much a part of human heritage for them to ever go away. Maybe they won't be used for work as much as they are now, but people will always find a piece of themselves in horses."

Ty let his gaze linger on his mother, taking in the determined set of her mouth and the fierce pride in her honey-colored eyes. Like everything else, she'd never been shy about professing her love of what their family did for a living, but it was rare that she was so poetic about it.

"That's just one of many, many reasons I have for wanting to see you and Shannon together. She's the one, Ty. She compliments you and she completes you."

"I'm well aware of that, Mom, but you know better than I do that relationships and marriage are two-way streets. I can't force her to feel the same."

"You think she doesn't? Take off the blinders, my boy."

"Are you and Shannon gonna get married?" young Hunter inquired, joining them in the kitchen to refill one of the sacks with colored icing. "I hope so. I like, Shannon."

"I know you do, sport," Ty replied. He glanced at his mother. Her expression was too nonchalant, and he suspected she'd signaled Hunter just in time for him to catch the end of their conversation. Turning to his nephew, he decided honesty was the best policy. "We'll see what happens, but don't get your hopes up too high just in case."

"But you want to marry her, right?"

"I'm pretty sure I do, yes."

"Glad to hear you admit that," Phoebe said under her breath.

"I've never actually denied how I feel about her," he retorted too quietly for Hunter to hear. He handed the boy the plate of cookies that had been cooling while the last batch was in the oven and said, "Here, take these to your mom and Shannon."

Ty held his tongue until his nephew was back at the table with his mother, siblings, and Shannon. The elder Hunter and Danny were in the office going over finances for the ranch, and Ty wished they were in here with the rest of the family to help him rein in Phoebe's plotting.

The scene at the dining room table—six kids ranging from the three-year-olds Seth and Rose to the eight-year-olds Hunter and Ant—were all smudged with colorful icing, and there was a mess of sprinkles and M&Ms all over the tabletop. It was nothing out of the ordinary for the Evans-Fitzwater clan, but Shannon's presence made the evening singularly special. Her wide-open smile and frequent laughter warmed his heart and made him ache for things he'd only begun to yearn for in the last couple years. Phoebe's blunt entreaties were annoying, yes, but they were also agonizing reminders that he couldn't just snap his fingers and make it happen.

"That's low," Ty asserted, returning his attention at last to his mother. "Recruiting your grandson to your cause. I know it's not your strongest trait, but a little patience would go a long way right now. Push either Shannon or me too hard before we're ready, and you might end up sabotaging your own scheme. You can't expect us to suddenly fall madly in love and get married and start working on a family in the space of a couple of weeks."

"You've been best friends for the better part of a decade, Ty."

"Yes, we have, but this whole idea of dating each other is still *very* new. Too new to be pushed." He loved her dearly, but he was well past obeying her every command, especially in situations that required a delicacy beyond her ability. "So don't push it."

She stared at him with her mouth open and her eyes round, and he almost regretted his sharp words. It wasn't often that he set boundaries with her, but he couldn't back down. So, without giving her a chance to recover her wits, he strode into the dining room and reclaimed his seat at the table.

He asked Shannon to pass him a snowflake cookie and the Ziploc baggie with the pale blue icing.

She leaned close as she handed the items over. "Everything all right?"

"Fine. Why?"

"Well, for one, *fine* usually means everything is *not*

fine. For another, you looked a little pissed a minute ago, while your mom looks, um, startled. So… what's going on?"

"Just Mom being Mom."

"She's pressuring you about us again, huh?"

Ty jerked his eyes from his cookie to her face, and it was his turn for his mouth to fall open in shock. "How…?"

"April said she's been bugging you about us since I've been back in Northstar."

"Lovely."

"It's okay, Ty. It's quite a compliment that she thinks so highly of me."

"She definitely thinks the world of you," he muttered. "And she isn't shy to admit it or remind me of it on a regular basis."

Shannon offered him a sympathetic smile. "I thought you'd appreciate that bit of knowledge. At least your mom likes me. Imagine how frustrating it'd be if she didn't. Instead of encouraging you, she'd be hindering you."

"You say that like you have experience with a boyfriend's mother who didn't like you. I thought Chris's mother adored you."

"I wouldn't use the word adored. She liked me well enough, and I don't think she would've had a problem with me marrying her son, but I never got the feeling that she *wanted* me in her family like your parents do. She was ambivalent, you could say, whereas your parents are decided. But I don't want to talk about Chris."

For the time being, he let that last bit slide. "Parents? Are you telling me Dad's been at it, too?" He glanced sharply at his sister.

April ducked her head sheepishly. "He might've said something to Shannon about her being the kind of woman he'd always hoped you'd settle down with."

"Dammit, Dad!" he called toward the office off the side of the dining room. "I expect that kind of direct attack from Mom, but you're usually more subtle."

The elder Hunter rolled his chair back from the desk and peeked through the door into the dining room, grinning broadly. "What can I say? I love the girl."

"Love you, too, Hunter," Shannon replied with a smile that matched his. She blew him a kiss.

"Traitors, the lot of you," Ty mumbled. He set his cookie and the icing down and headed for the front door. He didn't bother yanking his coat on before he stepped out into the frigid evening.

The sun had set only minutes ago, but with the thick ceiling of moody gray clouds, the only signal of it was a deepening of the gloom as night stealthily descended. He curled his hands around the railing, tipped his head back and chuckled. He wasn't in the least angry, but he wasn't going to give his family the satisfaction of hearing him laugh at their antics. The thrill that bubbled up with their overwhelming approval of Shannon was intoxicating, and even the icy wind that sliced through his thin flannel shirt and stole the warmth from his body couldn't kill the buzz.

The front door creaked open, and he tried with limited success to smother that tingling joy. Shannon joined him at the deck rail with concern in her enchanting eyes.

"Ty, are you…." Her words trailed off when he met her gaze and she noticed his smile. Playfully, she slapped his shoulder. "You brat. I thought you were angry."

"Why would I be angry? My family loves you, and what's more, you love them as much. Hell, you even seem to appreciate their meddling. What more could I hope for?"

He turned to her, slid his hands around her waist, and coaxed her into his arms, relieved when she let him.

"And yet you were upset with your mother earlier. Why?"

"Because, despite the fact that this is more real than anything I've ever felt, I still can't completely believe that we're *together* together. It's too new and fragile, and I don't want to break it by letting my impatient mother dictate how quickly we move."

She snuggled into him with her head on his shoulder and her arms tucked against his chest. She shivered, so he put his back to the biting wind to shield her from it. They stood like that for a long while, and Ty resolutely ignored the cold, unwilling to let her go.

"Ty, I need to tell you something," she said gently. "Celeste called while we were out on our ride with the kids to tell me Chris stopped by."

Ty straightened, every muscle in his body rigid. As firmly as Chris had closed the door on Shannon, there was only one reason why he'd want to see her—to open it again. "I may have only been to the Puget Sound area once, but I remember the time it takes to get from Seattle to Kingston. He didn't just *stop by*. He had a reason for going so far out of his way."

"He asked Celeste where I was. She thinks he might be thinking about getting back together."

Ty clenched his teeth. "And?"

"And that's it. She told him I was here visiting my brother, and he left."

"What if he *does* want to get back together?"

She leaned back in his arms, and it was his turn to shiver as a blast of cold air replaced the warmth of her body where they'd touched. The concern in her eyes and the accompanying wince dulled the fear her announcement evoked, and he brought her close again, holding her tightly to apologize for doubting her.

"I'm done with him."

"You're sure about that?" His words came out more cuttingly than he intended, so he inhaled and let it out slowly, and when he spoke again, his voice was gentler. "Three years is a lot of time to just throw away, and I'd understand—"

"He already threw it away." She met his gaze and held it. "I'm done with him, Ty, and moving on with you."

"And what if he decides to come out here to win you back?"

"He won't."

"Why not? I would. Haven't you considered why he 'stopped by' your house to see you?"

She shook her head.

"Something changed his mind, showed him that he was wrong, so no, I wouldn't put it past him to come all the way out here to get you back."

"It doesn't matter. If he fell for a lie once, he might fall for the same one again down the road." She shifted her weight and stepped back, hugging herself. "I don't want to talk about him anymore."

"That's fine, but if you want to put him behind you, you're going to have to open up and let it breathe someday."

"And what about you and Heather? Are you planning to let that open up and breathe someday, too? Or are you going to stand here and tell me you have zero regrets about that ending?"

"That's exactly what I'm telling you. She's a good friend, a hard worker, great with horses, and yes, a passionate lover. She's remarkable. No doubt about that. But even as much as she has that I want, she doesn't have it all." With his thumb under her chin and his chilled fingers resting against her neck and warmed enticingly by the heat of her soft skin, he tipped her head up and lowered his lips to hers. "You do. You've been my best friend long enough to know that I've never been invested enough in a relationship to have my heart broken. That's why I need to be certain you're sure about Chris—because I am now."

Saying it out loud eased the tension, and admitting not only to himself but also to Shannon that she had the power to hurt him deeply at least made his intentions and, he hoped, his devotion clear without fencing her in.

"I mean it, though, Shy Eyes. If Chris is the one who will make you happiest—I don't think he is anymore, but *if* he is—I won't stand in the way." He brushed a wayward strand of her hair out of her face. "Just please don't ask me to put on a smile and pretend I'm okay."

"I couldn't ever do that to you, Ty."

"Sure you could. Because it'd hurt me worse to see you unhappy." Draping an arm around her shoulders, he turned her back toward the house and intentionally didn't give her a chance to respond or himself the opportunity to dwell on the idea that her ex might very well show up in Northstar. "Let's not talk about it any more tonight. We still have a lot of cookies to decorate."

Five

BOTH THE BEDSPREAD INN'S restaurant and the game room in the basement were packed. Nearly every resident of Northstar had gathered around the two monster screens Pat and Aelissm had set up so everyone could watch together as the Montana State Bobcats fought in the semi-final playoff game for the chance to head to the national championship. While Montana college football was a popular pastime, even a playoff game with either the Cats or the Griz playing wouldn't have brought them all together, but this year, one of Northstar's own—June and Ben Conner's son Luke—would lead the Cats as the starting quarterback.

Shannon glanced around the crowded restaurant at the faces all turned toward the television, and the pride and love reflected in each kindled a bright glow in her heart. They could've been content to watch at home, but no, they'd come together to support a friend and neighbor even though he'd never know it unless someone told him. Northstar was a very special place, and she considered herself blessed to call it her second home.

Aelissm set two empty mugs on the bar in front of her. "Here you go, love. Go get your hot chocolate and get cozied up to that cowboy of yours again. Poor boy's looking a little lonely without you."

Shannon glanced over her shoulder at Ty, who was too busy chatting with his father, brother-in-law, and the three Hammond brothers to be lonely. "Just pitiful," she joked, turning back to her sister-in-law only long enough to thank her for the cups.

She filled the mugs with hot chocolate from one of the three hot beverage dispensers on the banquet table beside the side door and returned to her seat beside Ty. They'd arrived early enough to snag the more comfortable chairs usually gathered around the restaurants dining tables, and she was glad she didn't have to sit on one of the god-awfully uncomfortable metal folding chairs for the duration of the game.

Ty took the cup she held out to him, settled his free arm on the back of her chair, and beckoned her to scoot closer with a twitch of his fingers.

The topics of their conversation out on his parents' deck yesterday evening hadn't come up again, but they'd distracted her for almost the entire first half of the game.

If the score weren't displayed on the screen, she wouldn't have been able to tell anyone who asked who was winning. The Bobcats were up by only a point, and according to Ty's brother-in-law, Danny, it had so far been the best kind of game to watch—an edge-of-your-seat battle between two talented teams.

Ty's declaration yesterday that he was invested enough in their relationship to get his heart broken if it didn't work out conflicted with his assertion that he would step out of the way if Chris showed up wanting her back.

That's not exactly what he said. He said if Chris made me happy, he wouldn't try to stop it.

While she was touched by the sentiment that her happiness was of the utmost importance to him, she didn't know how to feel about him being unwilling to fight for her if she was truly the woman he wanted.

Doesn't matter, she told herself for the thousandth time. *Chris isn't coming back, and even if he does, I don't want him. I don't want someone who doesn't trust me.*

The thought that he might not only come crawling back to her but drive all the way to Northstar to do it was preposterous. Even when they'd been together, he'd hated the long drive out here. No, if he *were* of a mind to want her back—Ty's point about him going out of his way to see her the other day made too much sense for her to completely dismiss it—he'd wait until she came home. Her lips twitched into a faint smile. That possibility made staying here longer more appealing than it already was.

She threaded the fingers of her empty hand with Ty's and folded his arm around her, leaning into his side. Absently, he kissed the top of her head, and that simple gesture, so demonstrative of their undemanding bond, did a lot to loosen her tangled emotions. When the first half ended a few minutes later, she had pushed Chris from her thoughts again and committed herself to focusing on the man beside her. And what a handsome man he was, she mused as he tipped his face toward hers to kiss the tip of her nose.

"May I beg a favor?" he asked.

"Name it."

"Play a song for us?" He nodded his head toward the old upright piano behind the fireplace. "It's been a long time since I've heard you play."

"What song?"

"I couldn't care less."

Shannon nodded and wove her way to the piano through the crowd of people getting up to stretch. Ty followed her, sitting nearby on the flat stone lip of the fireplace to listen. She perched on the bench and held her fingers over the keys, flexing them for a moment while she decided which song to play. Settling on "God Rest Ye Merry Gentlemen," she took a deep breath and let her fingers dance over the keys at random for a moment to loosen up rusty skills. It hadn't only been a long time since Ty had heard her play the piano; it had been a long time since she'd played. A hush fell over the room when she began the song in earnest, and she closed her eyes to let the music flow through her and out her fingers. Never did she feel more graceful and competent than when she played any instrument, particularly a piano or a flute. The rest of the world fell away, and she became the notes and melodies and emotions.

She reached the end of the first song and moved seamlessly into her favorite, "Carol of the Bells," singing softly under her breath until her audience asked her to sing louder. Smiling broadly, she obeyed, and when she finished the song, she was met with enthusiastic applause. She started a third song—the more jovial "Holly Jolly Christmas," but Pat slid onto the bench beside her, slipping his hands beneath hers to take over the song. There had been a time when *he* had been the rusty one at the piano, but he needed no time to warm up, and she lifted her gaze to Aelissm, who watched them from behind the bar with a smile of the utmost adoration. Thanks to that remarkable woman, her brother had found the music Sara had tried—and nearly succeeded—to beat out of him.

"Why don't you ask Ty for a dance?" Pat whispered.

After only a moment's reluctance at having to let go of the music, she rose to her feet and held her hand out to Ty. Pat continued to play, and several couples got up to dance. At this particular moment, she was glad Northstar still clung to this tradition.

Ty eyed her hand with a brow lifted and a lopsided

smile. "Yes?"

"Dance with me?"

"You know I don't dance."

"Maybe it's time you learn." Grabbing his hand, she dragged him to his feet—something she couldn't have done if he didn't want her to. Half a foot taller than her at six-foot-one with a lean musculature built by his highly physical career, Ty outweighed her by almost sixty pounds. They slipped into each other's arms effortlessly and without hesitation, as comfortable with each other as ever.

"I wish you could see what I do when you play or sing, Shy Eyes," he murmured. "Nothing can compare to the beauty of it."

"Thank you." Startled by the praise, she shifted the focus off herself. "Are we going to dance or not? And no, that wasn't me giving you a choice."

"Good because I don't want one. But I do pity your poor feet," he teased. "I'm a total klutz on the dance floor."

"Many things you are, Tyger, but a klutz is definitely not one of them. Besides, I'm not looking for a complicated ballroom dance like some around us enjoy. I just want to hold you and be held by you."

"Do you now?"

"Mmm-hmm."

"I take this to mean you're warming up to the idea of us being together."

"I wasn't ever cold to it, but yes, I am. You're easy

to be with. Almost too easy because—and I've probably said this at least a dozen times—it's hard to tell if we're still just best friends or if we're actually moving forward."

"I can remind you that we're moving forward any time you like."

Without warning, he crushed her to him and dove after her neck so fast that she only just managed to keep the squeal of surprise locked in her lungs. Half a second later, an entirely different sound threatened to break loose as shivers coursed over every inch of her skin. Heat exploded in her core. The move and her reaction were definitely *not* the stuff of a platonic friendship, and when he reluctantly straightened, she understood that that was exactly the point he was trying to prove.

"A little more convinced now?" he asked in a low, husky voice that elicited another round of tingles. This was a side of Ty she'd never seen… and she liked it. A *lot*.

Unable to trust her voice, she nodded, biting her lip. With her arms threaded around his neck, she drew herself against his hard body and kissed him daringly. He held back, and after a moment, she leaned back with his hands folded lightly in the middle of her back in a subtle but powerful display of possessiveness and wished she could beg him for more, but it dawned on her that they were standing in a crowed room full of their friends and family. Many had turned curious and amused glances on them, and blush crept over her cheeks, so she buried her face against Ty's chest. That didn't help, and she let out a quiet squeak of mortification. He chuckled and hugged her.

"Enough dancing for a bit?" he inquired.

"I think so." Finally, she recovered enough to lift her head. "That was unexpected and… interesting."

"Just interesting?"

"No, a lot more than that, but this isn't the place to say what else."

Comprehension ignited in Ty's eyes alongside a distracting hunger.

There's the line I've been looking for, clear as crystal. And they were most definitely on the other side of it now.

As she absorbed that minute but momentous sliver of information, tranquility settled over her, stilling the restlessness that had been her constant companion since Ty had asked her on that first date. No, since he'd kissed her under the mistletoe two years ago.

He must have sensed the change because he brushed his lips across her cheek with a disarming tenderness and whispered, "Looks like we're on the same page now."

Then he stepped away and headed downstairs to check on April's kids so she didn't have to risk the steep stairs down to the basement. Shannon stared after him until he disappeared below her sight, then wandered over to her chair and sank onto it.

She had no idea how long she sat like that, staring blindly ahead, but it didn't seem like long before her brother lowered himself into the chair Ty had occupied during the football game.

"Care to dance with your old brother?"

Nodding, she pushed to her feet and stepped into Pat's arms. At some point, Aelissm had put on some music to fill the silence after her husband had ceased playing. The song was a slow Christmas tune, giving them plenty of time to talk as they danced.

"So tell me, sis. Do I need to break out the shotgun?"

"Huh?"

"You and Ty seem to be getting pretty close, and Mom and Dad made me sign a contract when you were born stating that it's my duty as your big brother to protect you."

"And you're good at it." She laughed softly. "The shotgun is more Aelissm's style, though."

"True enough. So, does my wife need to break out the shotgun? Personally, I don't think it's necessary. I trust Ty with you, but if you want her to, just say the word."

"I thought you trusted Chris, too."

"To a point. Until he took the word of someone who makes their living selling lies over yours, I thought he was a decent guy. Maybe a little too serious and uptight for you, but decent enough. You were happy with him, but if I may be frank...?"

She shrugged. "Might as well be."

"I stand by what I said. Ty has a gift for making you smile, and you're more relaxed with him than you were with Chris. A lot more. You have an incredible talent for sensing the moods of people around you. I think that's what makes you such a gifted singer and actress. You can soak it up and exude it and make everyone around you feel it, too. Do you get what I'm saying?"

She nodded. "Chris was uptight, so I was uptight. Ty is mellow, so I'm mellow. Or… mellower. I'm still unwinding a bit."

"Which is perfectly understandable, so give yourself a break."

They lapsed into silence, and while they danced, Shannon mulled over her brother's words. He was right, of course. As usual. It was also a relief to know that Ty had Pat's approval. She hadn't ever doubted that her brother liked him, but liking him as her friend and liking him as her prospective mate were two different realms because of the potential level of pain involved if things went south.

"Mind if I cut in?"

Shannon's spine snapped straight and ice lanced through her veins at the sound of his voice. Pat's expression turned dark, and she shuddered. She never wanted to see that shadow cross his beloved face again, but there it was, and it hit her heart hard.

"Get out of my restaurant," Pat said in a low, dangerous tone.

"Please, Pat, I just want to talk to Shannon. To apologize."

"No man *ever* calls my little sister what you did. Get. Out. Now."

"I'm sorry. I was an ass, and I was wrong. So wrong. Please just let me explain."

"No."

"Pat," Shannon whispered. She took his hand in both of hers and squeezed. "Let him talk."

His jaw clenched, but then he straightened and pointed a finger at Chris. "Hurt her again, and you'll wish you'd never set foot in here. I don't care if Aaron has to throw me in jail, I will *not* stand by and let you break my sister's heart again."

"Understood."

Shannon at last faced her ex. He stood a few feet away holding a huge bouquet of deep red roses like a shield. Two dozen, she figured without bothering to count them. She didn't want to talk to him, but she needed to, so she inclined her head toward the door and grabbed her coat off the back of her chair as she headed outside.

Seeing him again was harder than she'd imagined. He was undeniably handsome with thick dark hair, clear green eyes, and a groomed, urbanite masculinity that still made her heart trip with a primordial feminine appreciation. Ty, in contrast, still had a glimmer of boyish charm about the features of his face that softened the cowboy ruggedness of the rest of him. There was a wholly different kind of confidence in Chris's eyes than in Ty's, and after reacquainting herself with the latter over the past couple weeks, the former was a turnoff. Chris's confidence was more unabashed and rapacious whereas Ty's was, like him, gracious and unassuming.

"Why are you here, Chris?" she asked tiredly.

"Don't be like that, Shan."

She cringed at the nickname. So generic and unimaginative compared to Ty's Shy Eyes. "How should I be after what you called me?"

"Pissed, and rightly so, but give me a chance. Please."

"All right, fine. Talk."

First, he handed her the roses. "I brought these for you, hoping they might win me a little favor with you."

She took them and set them in the snow on the nearest picnic table, not really caring that the cold might bruise them. Chris winced, and she derived a perverse satisfaction from that.

"My friends think I'm nuts for coming out here," he continued, "but I couldn't wait until you came home. This is too important. I'm sorry. I never should've called you what I did, but damn, reading that article.… It hurt so much. I should've known it was a lie, but I couldn't see past the shock of it or how much it hurt. I'm so sorry for accusing you of being unfaithful and for not believing you."

"That's all well and good, but *why* the change of heart, Chris?"

"Macie and Kevin threatened the tabloid and the writer of the article with a libel suit, so they backtracked and published another story saying the first was a complete fabrication."

Shannon quirked a brow. Macie hadn't said anything about it when Shannon had called her the day before she'd talked to Celeste, and this kind of news was something she would have called about. Still, she didn't think Chris would lie about something like this.

"And Kevin sat down with me and made it pretty clear that there's never been anything but friendship between you and him… or him and any other woman, including his wife."

Chris definitely wasn't making *that* up. He'd have no reason to imagine anything like it; Kevin guarded that particular secret with a fervor that bordered on clinical paranoia. Shannon only knew it because she'd proven to him beyond a doubt that she could be trusted when he'd been asked point blank by a reporter early in their friendship if his male assistant was more than an assistant. The reporter claimed to have photo proof of them groping each other, and Kevin had floundered. Shannon had jumped in to dismiss the incident in question as nothing more than a drunken dare and reminded the reporter that Kevin had a wife he wasn't shy about displaying his affection for even in public. The image had later turned out to be very inconclusive, and the matter had been dropped.

"He told you?"

Chris nodded. "He cares deeply about you, Shannon, and he said he was sick that the tabloid gave me reason to doubt you. He wanted to set the record straight so I would know how much I hurt you when I didn't believe you."

God, this was hard. It had been hard enough to accept during that first couple of weeks that she and Chris were done, but now that he was here and saying these things, that time had been a proverbial cakewalk. All three years they'd spent together and all the fun and love of them came rushing back, and the pain of his rejection sharpened into a stabbing ache that made it difficult to breathe.

"So you know the truth now," she bit out. "What do you want?"

"I want to apologize for not believing you and to prove to you how sorry I am for what I said."

"And then what?"

"Then I hope you'll give us another chance. You're a wonderful woman, Shannon, and I don't want to lose you without a fight."

"You seemed pretty set on losing me when you called me a slut and told me to get out of your house."

"I was wrong." He reached to stroke her cheek, but she stepped back out of his reach. "Shannon….."

"What happens when the next lie is printed, Chris? Because if I pursue this career path, that one won't be the last."

"I'll believe you."

She couldn't trust that. That he was here in Northstar spoke volumes about his desire to win her back, but so too did the fact that it had taken the writer of the tabloid retracting his story and Kevin spilling his secret to convince Chris of her honesty. If he'd doubted her once, he might again.

"Shannon, please just give me a chance to show you I deserve another shot with you."

Folding her arms tightly around herself with her eyes burning, she shook her head and turned to head back inside, lifting her gaze just in time to catch Ty watching her with an expression laden with agony, anger, and disappointment. She opened her mouth to tell Chris no, but all that came out was a strangled groan as a tear spilled over. Memories of her time with Chris melded with the pain of his rejection and a desire for Ty's patience and jovial friendship into a wrenching straightjacket of confusion.

"Think about it?" Chris asked. "I have a few days off, but I'll take more if I need to."

Without giving any response at all and leaving the roses on the table, she wandered back inside, numbed by more than the December cold.

* * *

Ty crested the stairs, intent on begging Shannon for another dance before the game started up again, and stopped dead in his tracks when his gaze inadvertently caught sight of the view out the big windows straight ahead at the front of the restaurant. Shannon stood out on the broad deck talking to a man he'd met only twice, and at the sight of them, his heart dropped like a stone into a cold, deep, and empty well. He located Pat behind the bar, but Shannon's brother glared out the window with such ferocity that Ty didn't think the man would hear him.

"What the hell is Chris doing here?" Ty demanded of Aelissm instead even though two-dozen red roses lying in the snow on the picnic table was answer enough.

"Supposedly he came to apologize, but between you and me, I doubt he'd drive seven hundred miles just to say he was sorry. That's what phones are for."

"He wants her back," Ty muttered. "That son of a bitch."

"Agreed," Pat said. With conspicuous determination, the older man yanked his gaze from his sister and her ex and focused on Ty. "Looks like you were right about him showing up."

"Shannon told you I thought he would?"

Pat nodded. "I'm shocked he's here. He's not usually so quick to forgive."

"Forgive what? Shannon did nothing wrong. He's the one who screwed up."

"Once again we're in agreement, but although I would much rather knock his teeth in than attempt to understand him, I can unfortunately empathize with what he must've felt when he read the tabloid story. It's not pleasant to believe the person you love has been unfaithful, and if I had to describe it, I'd say it feels a bit like someone sticking a rusty knife in your guts."

Ty didn't consider for even a second Pat had ever suspected Aelissm of infidelity. "The bitch?"

At first, Pat's eyes widened in surprise, then he

shook his head and let out a huff of laughter. "I suppose I shouldn't be surprised Shannon's talked about Sara with you."

"That… and I was here the day she showed up. Even as a dumb teenager, I knew what she was."

With admirable composure, Pat put his anger at Chris away like he might put a coat away in the closet, locking it away out of sight. "I know this can't be any easier for you than it is for me, but right now she needs time and space to deal with this."

Ty nodded and swallowed hard, but the lump in his throat remained lodged in place. Pat squeezed his shoulder, and he met the other man's gaze.

"Trust her to make the right decision."

He replied only with a pinched and humorless smile, unable to muster anything more as hope came crashing down. How foolish he was to have thought Shannon might finally be his.

"Game'll be back on in a minute," Aelissm said with more gentleness than he usually associated with her. "I know it's too much to ask that you enjoy it, but try, all right?"

"I'll try," he croaked.

The second half kicked off before Ty made it back to his chair. His father leaned over and asked if he was all right, nearly drowned out by the cheer that rose when Luke launched a Hail Mary pass on the Bobcats' first possession of the half to his receiver in the end zone. Glad it was too loud for his answer to be heard, because his voice would certainly betray the lie, he nodded. Try as he might, he couldn't keep himself from glancing over his shoulder out the windows.

Trust her to make the right decision. He repeated Pat's words over and over again, but they did little to assuage the dread. Though he and Shannon had been friends for close to a decade, he wasn't sure their romantic relationship could compete against the three years she'd been with Chris, and the fear that he'd once again be relegated to the friend zone was very real.

He glanced outside yet again, and while she was too far away for him to be sure, she looked like she was about to cry. Anger burned away the fear and dread, but he held it in check until she walked inside and lowered herself mechanically into the chair beside him and he saw the track of a single tear shining on her cheek. Explosive fury consumed him, and one more glance out the window at Chris's smug face had him shooting out of his chair.

Shannon uttered his name, begged him to come back. He kept walking.

"Ty!" Pat called, jogging around the bar to stop him. "Don't do it! Ty, please!"

Other voices echoed the same all around him, but he ignored them and stormed outside. "You're a real piece of shit, Chris, you know that? You are not worthy of her."

Chris pointedly looked him up and down with his lip curled in a sneer. "And you are?"

"Maybe not, but I'm a damned sight better than

you. I would've taken her word about the tabloid."

"You can't say that. You didn't see the picture or read the article."

"I don't need to see it or read it. If she said it's a lie, I'd believe her because I know her and I trust her to tell me the truth."

The man had the audacity to laugh. "So says the man who kissed *my* girlfriend two years ago, too drunk to respect her boundaries. Yeah, you're a great one to teach me a lesson about trust and honor."

"You're right, I'm not, and the blame for that kiss lies entirely on me. If you were half the man you think you are, you would've accepted that. But you didn't. No, you used that kiss as evidence against her as if she did something wrong." Ty's hand clenched into a fist. What he wouldn't give to strike that arrogant smirk right off her ex's face, but he wouldn't be the one to throw the first punch. *Come on, asshole. You know you want it. You've wanted to hit me since that night.*

"And I've since learned how wrong I was."

Ty's gaze sidetracked briefly to the roses. His temper burned hotter with the thought that Chris believed he could buy Shannon's forgiveness rather than earn it. "Yeah? How'd you figure that out?"

"How doesn't matter."

"Wrong. It matters a *lot*. Because you're either a decent guy who had a gut-check moment and figured out that she's as loyal as they come, or you're a jackass who only came to that conclusion because he was led to it.

Which is it, Chris?"

Seconds ticked by, but Chris didn't respond, stubbornly gritting his teeth. That was all the answer Ty needed.

"That's what I thought. You're a jackass." He shook his head and started to walk away, but hesitated. "For the record, I wasn't drunk."

"Excuse me?"

"When I kissed Shannon. Kinda hard to get drunk without having a single drink." Ty turned methodically around. Understanding widened his companion's eyes. "And it wasn't an accident that I—"

Chris's fist connected with his jaw, snapping his head around. Ty's mouth curled in a feral grin, and he struck back, landing a punch to his opponent's cheek fast and hard enough to knock him down. Chris sprawled on his back in the snow. Gratification licked deliciously through Ty, satiating the raging desire for a fight and the pent-up need to defend Shannon from further callous treatment at Chris's hands. A tiny voice in the back of his mind whispered that he'd regret this later, but he ignored it.

"You don't want to fight me, boy," he snarled, flexing his hand. "I make my living wrangling animals a lot bigger and a lot stronger than you."

The bell on the door jingled, but he didn't look to see who'd come outside.

"Jesus Christ, Ty!" Shannon snapped, dropping to Chris's side. She turned accusing eyes on him. "What the hell was that for?"

With those words, *later* became *right now*. Ty opened his mouth to respond, but nothing came out. Anger melded with bitter betrayal and agonizing heartbreak as she knelt in the snow and cradled Chris's head in her hands. Chris grunted as he sat up with Shannon's assistance and prodded the back of his head. When she tilted his head to inspect his cheek, Ty stormed away. He stepped inside just long enough to grab his coat, turning a deaf ear to the inquiries about what had happened. He took a step toward the door, but jerked to a halt when Heather planted herself in front of him.

"Maybe it isn't what it looks like," she said gently.

"And maybe it's *exactly* what it looks like."

"I've never known you to jump to conclusions." She opened her arms, and he let her hug him tightly, grateful for even that tiny bit of support from a friend. "Don't start now."

She released him. He stepped around her and rushed out to his truck. Slamming the door closed, he gunned the engine to life and sped out of the crowded parking lot with his tires spinning in the snow and his truck fishtailing.

Back at his cabin, he locked the door, drew the curtains closed, and turned on the game, then paced the living room, too agitated to sit still and watch the Bobcats claw their way to a secure lead. He'd been home barely fifteen minutes and had only just adjourned to the couch with it becoming apparent that his shaking legs wouldn't be capable of holding him up much longer when he heard someone climbing the steps to his deck. A moment later, a knock sounded on his door, but he made no move to see who was on the other side. He didn't have to; he sensed it in the marrow of his bones.

"Ty, I know you're home. Please open the door."

The regret in Shannon's voice cracked his heart a little more, compelling him to go to her, but he remained seated. The image of her jumping to Chris's defense was agonizingly clear in his mind's eye and paralyzed him.

"Please, Ty."

He said nothing and made no move toward the door, and after a few minutes, he heard her walking down the stairs. He hunched over his knees with his arms curled around his head, unable to clear that image from his mind. His jaw and the knuckles of his right hand hurt, but they were nothing compared to the ache in his chest. Whatever choice she made, he'd have to live with it. *Trust her to make the right decision,* Pat had said. Ty promised himself he'd do just that because he *did* trust her, but the question was… *right for whom?*

Six

THE FOLLOWING MORNING dawned clear and bright with the sun sparkling on the carpet of fresh, perfect snowflakes. Certain Ty would have been up before the sun, Shannon encased herself in her winter gear and headed out to her car, which she'd started a quarter of an hour ago to let it warm up in the bitterly cold morning. She would have preferred to walk over to the Bar E and let the endorphins released by the exertion settle her nerves, but after Ty had refused to answer his door yesterday afternoon, she wasn't certain he would want to talk to her, and she didn't want to brave the subzero temperatures for nothing if that was the case.

She drove around to the Bar E's main driveway and glanced up at his house as she passed it. There was no sign of life other than the slender curl of smoke drifting from the chimney, and the snow had been swept from his deck and stairs, confirming that he'd already headed to work, but when she parked beside the barn, there was no sign of him. Her SUV's dash thermometer read minus twenty-one, so maybe he was in the pavilion. With a bundle of nerves unlike any that had ever plagued her where Ty was concerned, she climbed out of her car, stuffed her hands in her pockets, and strode around the barn to the side door of the big pavilion. She entered quietly. It wasn't much warmer inside than out, but sheltered from the elements, it *felt* warmer. Christmas music played over the stereo system Ty had had installed shortly after the pavilion had been erected, but it was turned down too low to cover the rhythmic thumps of a horse's hooves moving through soft dirt or the animal's huffed breaths.

Her eyes adjusted from the blinding snow to the dim light filtering through the skylights and high windows, and there he was, loping the magnificent black Arabian colt with neither saddle nor bridle in figure eights in the soft dirt. At the moment, he was absorbed by his work, and the pure joy of it washed over his features, making him at once more devastatingly handsome than Chris could ever hope to be. Though he'd only been working with Shadow for a couple weeks now, the changes in the young stud were plain even to her untrained eye. The Arabian *wanted* to please Ty, and even when his rider needed to use a firmer hand than he would with Holly or another horse he'd been training for longer, it was clear that he was trying.

After a flawless set of flying lead changes, Ty grinned and brought the colt to a halt, then leaned forward over his neck, stroking his hand down the animal's glossy fur and whispering something Shannon was too far away to hear. Whatever it was, Shadow obviously liked it. His ears swiveled to catch Ty's every word.

He straightened again and noticed Shannon standing in the shadows. His face darkened as an emotion she couldn't name contorted his expression. For the first time in the long history of their friendship, she got a glimpse of another side of Ty, but unlike the startlingly passionate side he'd revealed yesterday before Chris had showed up, this was one she didn't want to become familiar with.

"Hello, Ty," she greeted hesitantly.

"Shannon."

"Did you catch the rest of the game?"

He nodded, but she doubted he'd paid much attention to it.

"The Bobcats are headed to the national championship. How incredible for Luke, huh?"

"Yep." He slid off Shadow's back and strode over to the big door at the end of the pavilion closest to the lower pasture. With uncharacteristically jerky movements, he rolled the door open.

"Shadow's beginning to look like a veteran instead of a green-broke colt. I'm amazed at how fast he's picking this up, but you always said Arabians are remarkably intelligent."

Ty turned abruptly toward her with impatience radiating from him, and she took a step back, stunned.

"Why are you here, Shannon?"

"Because you're my friend and because we need to talk about what happened yesterday."

"So talk. I'm not in the mood to play games."

"Obviously," she teased.

The expression he leveled at her was anything but amused.

"Why did you hit Chris?"

"Maybe you didn't see it, but he hit me first. As to why I hit him back, someone has to stand up to him for you because you apparently won't."

That stung. "I'm perfectly capable of handling my own affairs."

"I know you are, but just because you can doesn't mean you should *have* to all the time. It broke my heart to see you upset."

"Why does it matter so much to you?" As soon as the words were out of her mouth, she wished she could take them back. With that tactless question, she had completely marginalized every embrace, every laugh and smile, and every kind word he'd ever uttered to her, too ignorant and self-absorbed to acknowledge how much he cared about her as if what he felt meant nothing.

He spun on her with his brows drawn tight and low over his eyes. "Do you really not get it?"

"Get what, Ty?"

He stared at her for a moment, then shook his head

and launched onto Shadow's back. He wheeled the horse around and heeled the colt with more force than she'd ever seen him use—a testament to how angry he was. *No, how hurt*, she corrected, flinching as Shadow lunged forward with a startled grunt. She hugged herself and watched horse and rider charge away through the snowy pasture with their breath turning to clouds of silver and Shadow's hooves churning the powder into glistening plumes. Were it not for the anger or disappointment or whatever it was stiffening Ty's usually graceful body, the sight would have topped her list of the most breathtaking things she'd ever seen. Instead, the scene wavered as tears filled her eyes, and hugging herself tightly, she raced back to her car, slipping and stumbling in her haste.

Back in the warmth of her vehicle, she let out a plaintive whine as the first tears trickled down her cold cheeks. What was happening? Ty had been such a reliably even-keeled presence in her life for so long that his chilly reception left her unbalanced as her world tilted.

She had to fix this. But how could she when she didn't understand why he was so upset? She went over everything that happened yesterday—their dance and the moment she'd recognized they had undeniably left the friend zone behind, Chris's revelations, Pat's plea that she let Ty and Chris settle their issues alone, and running back outside just in time to see Chris go down. It had never before crossed her mind that Ty could hit so hard, and the shock of it still resonated through her.

Pain rattled through her head when her forehead

smacked the steering wheel.

She'd checked to see if Chris was all right first, leaving Ty to seek solace with Heather for a moment before he'd abruptly departed. In her mind, it had been obvious that Ty was fine while her ex wasn't, but to him and Heather, it must've seemed like she was choosing Chris over Ty. And in a moment of brilliant clarity, she had the answer to the question of why this mattered so much to Ty.

Oh, God.

She really was blind. All those lightly uttered comments about thinking about her differently since their kiss and that almost teasing conversation about him hoping she'd be the one to help him make a family of his own. Those playful remarks weren't his way of testing what he felt; they were hints to help her catch up. Then there was what he'd said Friday about being in a position to have his heart broken. She groaned. There was only one reason his heart would be in jeopardy.

Ty wasn't merely curious to see if he *could* love her. He already *did*.

With a renewed threat of tears, she prayed she hadn't destroyed their friendship with her thoughtless actions.

I have to fix this, she thought again. *I don't want to lose him.*

Where did she start? The same confusion that had prevented her from saying no to Chris yesterday was still there. The habits of their time together were strong, but so was the memory of how easily he'd dismissed her, and yes, she still had residual feelings for him—there had been and still was a strong enough pull to keep them together for so long—but her time with Ty had significantly diminished them. Their most recent interactions notwithstanding, being with him in any capacity was effortless. She never felt self-conscious with him like she often did in the presence of Chris's seriousness.

If someone told her she had to choose right then and there with no deliberation, which man would she pick if she couldn't see the other ever again?

Ty.

No hesitation whatsoever. The thought of her life without him in it brought a sharp, physical pain like someone had stabbed her with a cold iron spike, and that was the only proof she needed to know that he was the right choice. Her relationship with Chris was broken, and she didn't need to set the record straight. She didn't need closure. She needed to repair the damage she'd done to her friendship with Ty by believing for even a moment that she owed Chris a chance to explain himself, and having her ex here was only going to distract her from that task.

That's where she'd start. She'd tell Chris to go home.

She wiped under her eyes with her thumb, put her SUV in gear, and drove away from the Bar E. When she reached Elkhorn Road, she turned right toward the Bedspread instead of left toward her cabin. Chris had checked into a room at the inn, and though she was shocked her brother had agreed to let him stay there, it would make things easier. If Chris didn't want to leave, Pat would gladly kick him out.

Shannon parked by the stairs at the end of the inn and inhaled as deeply as the icy air allowed before she ascended to the second floor. Chris was in the room closest to the top, and after hesitating only a single thud of her racing heart, she knocked. She heard shuffling within, and a moment later, Chris opened the door wearing only a pair of sweat pants that hugged his narrow hips and long legs. Not so long ago, the sight of his cut upper body would have set her pulse to hammering, but now it was only nerves and anxiety that had it racing.

"You've been crying," he said in place of a greeting.

With her eyes undoubtedly red from her tears, there was no point in denying it. "Yes, I have. I may lose one of my best friends over this, and if I do, I'll deserve to lose him."

"Why would you lose him?"

Chris's tone wasn't overly probing, but she sensed he'd chosen his words carefully to draw out of her a denial of whatever Ty had said to him yesterday. What *had* Ty said to provoke him?

"I hurt him, Chris. That's why I might lose him."

His eyes narrowed briefly, and undoubtedly he read *something* into her statement, but he didn't press her about it. Instead, he opened the door farther and stepped back to let her enter. She shook her head, declining the invitation. She'd done enough damage already. The last thing she needed was a citizen of Northstar spotting her going into Chris's room and reporting it to Ty.

"Please come in, Shannon. We're going to freeze standing here."

"I don't want to talk right now. I'm not sure I can. I stopped by to ask you to dinner tomorrow evening so we can talk then."

"Why do we have to wait until tomorrow? Why don't I take you out to breakfast instead? Or dinner tonight."

She shook her head. It probably wasn't a good idea to let Ty stew about this for too long, but even tonight would be too soon for her to properly work her way through this mess, and at any rate, she already had plans. "I'm watching my brother's kids tonight."

"Bring them with."

Wow. He *was* determined. "No, Chris. Not today."

"Why not? It's not like you have anything pressing to do. You're on vacation, right?"

"Not right now, Chris," she repeated again. "I need some time to put my thoughts together before we talk. Meet me at the Ramshorn tomorrow at five? You remember how to get there, right?"

"I remember. I wish you wouldn't make me wait so long to see you again."

She ignored that. "I'll see you tomorrow. Until then, please leave me alone."

Sensing that her shaky grip on her emotions was

about to fail, she turned away and strode toward the stairs with her back straight, consciously monitoring her breathing to keep it from quickening into shallow, panicky gulps.

"Shannon."

With her foot hovering over the precipice of the step, she glanced over her shoulder and waited for him to speak again.

"I love you."

The tender entreaty in his voice triggered her habit to say it back, but she pressed her lips together in a sad smile to keep the words trapped inside. The sincerity in them had fractured the moment he'd told her to leave his house, and without it, the words were hollow and fizzled quickly. She turned away, gingerly descending the stairs to her car feeling so fragile that she was certain obeying her urge to flee would shatter her. Deciding to close the door on Chris didn't make the act any easier to do. Yes, he'd hurt her, but she *had* loved him.

* * *

"Thanks for coming by today."

Heather dipped her head in a nod of acknowledgement and took out her Leatherman to clip the twine on the first bale of hay stacked on the flatbed of the ranch's feed truck. With his pitchfork, Ty began tossing hay to the Bar E's fifteen impatient Angus heifers and their calves.

"Didn't feel like being alone after yesterday's scuffle, hmm?" Heather inquired, grabbing the extra pitchfork after she'd cut the twine on the rest of the bales.

"I asked you to come because Danny's under the weather," he replied. "But yes, it's nice to have some friendly company right now."

"And why isn't Shannon here to keep you company?"

"Do you really need to ask? You saw the whole thing."

"Maybe I want to hear you explain it."

"She chose Chris."

"And you're going to let it go at that?"

"Believe me, Heather, I don't want to, but I can't force her to do something she doesn't want to no matter how much it hurts me to watch her love someone else. I care too much about her to try to cage her like that."

"You're a dumbass."

Ty gritted his teeth and forked more hay to the cows without responding.

"I didn't let a great guy go just to watch him make a mess with the woman who is the reason why he can't love me."

Her choice of phrase caught his attention, and he leaned on his pitchfork to peer at her with eyes narrowed. "You lied."

"Not entirely. I'm not ready for what you want."

"How about the part that we were barely more than friends?"

"Also true, but that doesn't mean I wasn't coming around and finding more and more to appreciate about you every day."

"You know what they call that, right?"

"No. Enlighten me."

"Settling."

She gave a snort of laughter. "No woman would ever be settling for you, Ty. Me included. She might have to open her eyes and see what a rare find you are, but she'd never have to settle."

He appreciated that she was trying to soothe his bruised ego, but it wasn't his ego that needed lulling, and her words had the opposite of the intended effect. He felt like he'd failed her, too. "This isn't making me feel any better, Heather. In fact, it's making me feel guilty as hell."

"Why? Because I'm a silly girl who still wants to have fun? I'll find the right man for me someday… if I decide that's what I want. In the meantime—" She poked his deltoid hard enough to make him yelp. "—don't let your right woman slip away."

Sighing, Ty got back to work. They finished their task quickly and climbed back into the truck. He gripped the steering wheel with both hands side by side at the top and his knuckles white. He parked the flatbed in front of the barn for the time being, and climbed out. His arm was still sore, and he rubbed it, glaring at Heather without anger. With the afternoon chores completed, it was time for her to leave, so he walked with her over to her car, which was parked out of the way beside the corral beneath the big Doug fir.

He heard a vehicle approaching but for the time

being didn't look to see who it was. "Thanks for the help this afternoon. I needed it."

She embraced him, and he held on to her longer than he should, glad for the support. He missed her when she slipped away, but before she slid into her truck, she kissed his cheek, then let her hand linger on his arm—the same one she'd poked—for a moment in an unspoken invitation to lean on her if he needed a friend again. He hooked his thumbs in his front pockets and watched her drive away.

It was then that he remembered the other vehicle, a high-end black sedan with tinted windows. He didn't recognize it, and glancing at the Washington plates, his first thought was of Shadow's owners, but he wasn't expecting them for another two weeks.

Chris.

Ty didn't wait for him to get out of his ritzy car. With fury licking through him, ready to explode at the lightest provocation, he marched toward the barn.

"Hey, Evans!" Chris called after him.

"Get the hell off my ranch, Delarose."

"I'm not here to fight with you. I'm here to offer a truce."

Ty stopped and tipped his head back, debating the wisdom of engaging in *any* conversation with Shannon's... ex? Boyfriend? He didn't know. He started walking again.

"Please, Ty. I'm here for Shannon's sake. She's torn up over what happened yesterday. We're going to have to deal with each other because we both love her, so let's set our differences aside right here and now."

False, taunting words. Every damned one Chris uttered. Ty kept walking, but Chris followed him into the barn. Ty did his best to ignore him, finding any excuse to do so—straightening tack in the tack room, topping off the barn cats' food and water bowls that were still nearly full from when he and Heather had come through less than an hour ago, sweeping a floor that didn't need to be swept. To his dismay, Chris didn't take the hint.

"I'm taking Shannon to dinner tomorrow night, and I'd like to be able to tell her we're good and that she won't have to worry about any more incidences like yesterday."

"You're taking her to dinner?" He pinched his eyes closed for a moment and reminded himself of his promise to abide by whatever decision Shannon made. He would not stand in the way of her happiness, even if that meant stepping out of Chris's way.

"Yes, tomorrow evening at the Ramshorn. We're getting back together."

Chris's voice was too smug, and Ty glanced over his shoulder to meet a gaze too intently unwavering. Beneath that combative glint, however, doubt shimmered. It was possible that Shannon was in fact going to dinner with him, but Chris had no idea if she wanted to get back together with him.

He wasn't here to offer a truce.

Ty grabbed the saddle he'd oiled this morning off

the stand beside the tack room and returned it to its rack, completing the absolute last task. With nothing left to distract him, he faced Chris, standing just inches from him. Satisfaction flickered when the other man leaned back a fraction of an inch. "You need to grow up, Chris."

"Come again?"

"Did I stutter?" Ty enunciated. "You came here to brag like a little boy who cares about nothing but that he won. When you figure out that Shannon is not a toy to be bagged in some bullshit schoolyard game, come back and talk to me. Until then, you are trespassing."

He was late for dinner with his family, so he switched off all the lights in the barn but the one over the man door. Chris remained where he was.

"Are you deaf?" Ty shoved against the man's chest, pushing him out the door. "Leave."

Chris's hands balled into fists, and adrenaline rippled through Ty's veins. For several tense seconds, he hoped the other man might give into the rage that flashed in his eyes.

Understanding mingled with the pulse of exhilaration. There would be no truce between them. Ever. The ramifications of that truth curled icy talons into him, and he longed for an outlet for the poisonous vapor of fury and grief.

"Do it," he growled. "*Please.*"

His words broke the spell. Chris whirled away, jumped in his shiny car, and sped down the driveway, splattering Ty with snow.

Methodically, Ty brushed the snow from his clothes. Then he let out a bellow that left his vocal chords stinging and slammed the barn door, angered anew by what this situation was bringing out of the depths of him.

He was already late for dinner with his family, thanks to Chris's childish chest beating, so he stomped down the driveway to their house. The walk wasn't enough to cool his temper sufficiently, so he sat heavily on the top step with his elbows braced on his knees and scrubbed his hands through his hair. After a moment, he lifted his gaze from this boots to the darkening sky. In his foul mood, he'd missed the sunset, and with those long streamers of cirrus decorating the sky, it should have been too spectacular for him to ignore. He let out a strangled growl. He wasn't like this. Wasn't this intemperate beast.

The front door creaked open, but he didn't look to see who now stood on the deck behind him.

"Ty?" his sister inquired gently. "What are you doing out here?"

"Listing all the reasons why tracking Chris down and beating him senseless is a monumentally stupid idea."

She sat gently beside him and dropped her head to his shoulder. "That's a long list."

"Not long enough."

"Shouldn't you have let this go by now?"

"You tell me."

He repeated his brief and stilted conversation with Shannon this morning and what Chris had said along with his observations and perceptions of the whole mess. April withheld her usual sisterly teasing and listened quietly without interrupting. He admitted that he was afraid Shannon had chosen Chris, and his voice trembled. She pulled his head down to her shoulder, dousing the writhing hunger to fight and leaving him hollow and cold.

"My poor little brother," she murmured. Her words were patronizing, but her sympathetic tone negated them. "This is quite a knot you've gotten your heart into. But don't give up yet. Shannon's always struck me as a smart woman who wouldn't be fooled by a simple apology and a couple dozen roses. She'll want proof that he won't hurt her again, and that'd take a lot longer than twenty-four hours."

He mulled over every event since yesterday for the hundredth time, and when he came to that moment on the deck of the Bedspread when Shannon had dropped to Chris's side without so much as a glance or a gesture to see if Ty was all right, he wanted to kick himself for letting his anger get the best of him. There was no doubt in his mind about who'd started the fight. Sure, he'd been rightly furious at Chris's mistreatment of Shannon, and he'd had no hope of fighting the instinct to defend her, but he'd let two years of pent-up frustration get the better of him. It pained him, but in Shannon's place, he would've been disappointed in him, too.

He straightened but let April tuck her arm around his waist and scoot close for warmth as a biting wind wafted in from the north. "What happened after I left?"

"Well… Chris wouldn't let Shannon help him up. I don't think he expected you could knock him on his ass, and he was pretty pissed about it. Then he checked into a room at the Bedspread, and that was the last anyone saw of him that I know of. Shannon left almost right after you did. She wanted to come talk to you, but I told her not to because I figured you needed some space to cool down. Now I think I may have been wrong to tell her that. Did she stop by or did she just go home?"

"She stopped by… and I didn't answer the door." Ty grimaced. "I screwed up, April. I lost sight of what's important."

"No, you didn't, and if she can't see that, maybe she's not the girl you think she is."

"Maybe not, but she's still the only one I want."

"Then you might find this encouraging, or at least interesting." April tightened her arm around him. "Those roses Chris brought? She left them sitting on the table in the snow."

Seven

SHANNON INTENTIONALLY ARRIVED at the Ramshorn's lodge half an hour before she'd told Chris to meet her there in case he had the idea to swing by her cabin to ride with her. She needed to make it very clear that this was not a date. Of course, her early arrival would give her far too much time to overthink everything she planned to say.

The jingle of the bell on the door as she stepped inside the lodge needled her already hypersensitive nerves, but as her eyes adjusted from the bright outdoors to the dim interior, that minor torment ebbed. Fake pine garlands studded with clear mini lights and accented with festive red satin bows were draped around the room and added a healthy touch of holiday cheer, as did the crackling fire in the hearth, the elegant Christmas tree in the far corner trimmed primarily in red, white, and gold, and the Santa hat on the black bear beside the door. What a welcome change from the penetrating cold and gloomy gray of impending snowfall outside.

"Well, look who it is. It's about time I get to see you."

She turned her head to the familiar voice and grinned as her anxiety over her impending sit-down with Chris evaporated. Luke Conner sat on a stool at the thick, log-slab counter holding his seven-month-old sister, Corrie, and chatting with his parents. She half-ran to him with arms out-stretched, and he shifted his sister to one hip and wrapped Shannon in a one-armed bear hug.

"It's so good to see you!" she greeted when he released her. "But how come I haven't seen you before now? And why are you home on a Monday? Don't you have practice tonight?"

"Today's the first day in a month that I've been able to make it home. No classes today, so we had practice this morning, and I decided to drive home for the evening. I'll head back to Bozeman first thing in the morning."

She stood back to inspect him. "You were right, June," she said to Luke's mother without glancing at her. "He *does* look better. A little tired, maybe, which is completely understandable, but happier. Of course, winning the semi-final might explain it, but I hope it's more lasting than that. Congratulations, by the way."

"Don't congratulate me yet," Luke replied. "We still have one more game to play."

"You're saying I can't congratulate you for *making* it to that last game?"

"If you must."

He laughed, and it gave her hope. If he could find joy and amusement in life after what he'd been through, she could certainly find the courage to face Chris. He returned to his stool, and she perched on the one beside him. Corrie reached for her.

"Want to take her, Shannon?" Luke asked.

"Only if her big brother doesn't mind."

"I get to see her a lot more than you do."

Shannon took the infant from her brother. "Hi, baby girl. My goodness you've grown since I saw you in Washington this summer."

Time sped by as she talked with him and June and Ben about the national championship, Luke's plans for the rest of his final year of college and beyond, and her indecision over her career. Occasionally, either Ben or June would step away to greet a customer, deliver food to diners, or check guests in to cabins, but the love of their family, which enfolded her in a protective cocoon of peace, remained uninterrupted. She counted herself blessed that her brother's marriage to Aelissm had brought not only his wonderful if occasionally sarcastic wife into her life but also the Conners because they had become as much a part of her life as any blood relation… if not closer.

The bell jingled again, and Shannon glanced toward the door to see Chris stroll into the lodge. Dressed in crisp new blue jeans and what appeared to be a deep green V-neck sweater beneath a plain but stylish black parka with a black knit hat covering most of his dark hair, he was casually but breathtakingly sexy. His brows briefly dipped when his eyes landed on Luke, and his comment about her having a "thing" for June and Ben's son came to mind. She bristled at the memory.

"Merry Christmas, Conner family," Chris greeted.

"Same to you," June responded politely.

"Great game on Saturday."

"Thanks," Luke replied. He flicked his gaze to Chris and quirked a brow at Shannon as he took his sister back from her. Of course he would have heard about everything by now.

Subtly, she shook her head in answer to his unspoken inquiry, then excused herself from the Conners, grabbing two menus on her way to the table beside the Christmas tree.

"And here I thought I was early," Chris said, moving to pull her chair out for her.

She beat him to it, intent on maintaining her boundaries. Shrugging, he leaned down to kiss her cheek and took the chair across from her, and she handed him a menu, trying hard not to curl her lip in annoyance. As she pretended to study her menu, the absurdity of spending an entire meal with him dawned on her. What she needed to say wouldn't take that long, and giving him that much of her time would only make this more difficult than it already was and give him a chance to try to reopen a door she wanted to lock permanently.

While he looked over his menu, she studied him. There was a sophisticated poise in his posture that contrasted the Conners' relaxed poses, and once it had captivated her. Now it served only to remind her that she'd always been not on edge, exactly, but a touch wired in his presence, and her time in Northstar with her brother and his family, Ty and his, and now the Conners had shown her that that wasn't the Shannon she wanted to be. She wanted to be the fun-loving, unperturbed Shannon she was here with them.

Still, she and Chris had been together for a long time, and the things that had drawn her to him and kept her with him hadn't gone away.

She set her menu on the table. "You know what? This is silly. I need to just get this over with."

"Get what over with?"

"This. Us."

He folded his hands with his elbows braced on the table and rested his chin on them, meeting her gaze head on with a light, confident smile playing about his eyes and lips. Her heart fluttered, and she wished she could say it was only nerves that made it do so.

Oh, for the love of God! Focus, Shannon.

"I accept your apology," she said slowly.

"That's good. I am—"

"But I can't take you back."

He snapped his mouth closed and frowned in confusion. "Just like that? You're not even going to give me the benefit of the doubt?"

"Like you gave *me* the benefit of the doubt?"

"Please don't do this. I love you."

"If you loved me, you wouldn't have doubted me."

"I'm sorry. How many times do I have to say it? What do I have to do to prove how sorry I am?"

"You don't have to prove anything. I get that you're sorry. The fact that you're here says everything I need to know."

"But it's not enough."

"No."

For a long time, he didn't respond, just stared at her with a frown drawing his brows low over his eyes and the muscle in his jaw working. Slowly, his expression softened until his eyes drooped with resignation. She wanted to see anger or disappointment or even regret. Anything but resignation. Chris wasn't the kind to give up, and she hated to see that shadow in his eyes. Even more, she hated to be the cause of it. She might not want to rekindle their romance, but she didn't want to break him. Perhaps that was his intent, to entice her loyal nature into making her cave.

"There's nothing I can do?" he asked with such tenderness in his voice that she squirmed.

"I'm sorry, Chris, but no."

He sighed and pressed his lips into a flat line, held her gaze a moment longer, and then picked up his menu again. Deep in the far corner of her mind, she was aware that she was a piano being played by a master.

June came over to take their orders, and after she left, Chris kept her busy with small talk about the movie deal, about Luke's upcoming game, even about the weather, and Ty's horses. The shift in topic to Ty was so subtle that she didn't notice until he was asking about a pretty young brunette. By his descriptions, she immediately knew he was talking about Heather.

"Is she Ty's girlfriend?"

"Not anymore," Shannon replied warily. "She still works for him, though."

"She's stunning. So natural and confident. A lot like you, but much less shy about it." He sipped his glass of merlot. "You're sure they're not still dating?"

"Positive. She broke up with him a few weeks ago."

His shrug was a little too nonchalant, and with it, the architecture of his seemingly harmless small talk suddenly became apparent to Shannon.

"Where were you to see them together?" she asked in a carefully controlled voice.

"Out at his ranch."

"*What* were you doing at the Bar E?"

"I went over to offer a truce. I had hoped that maybe, if I could show you that he and I could settle our issues, you would see how much I care about you. I'm sure by now it's no secret that I don't care for him, but I'm willing to set that aside for your sake."

It might reveal too much about why she was closed

to getting back together with him, but she couldn't stop herself from asking, "Why do you think they're back together?"

"I don't know. They just seemed a little closer than friends… or boss and employee, I guess it is."

Shannon started to deny it, but then she remembered how Heather had hugged Ty after his fight with Chris.

"Ty's the real reason you won't give me another chance," Chris surmised.

She didn't answer, but her silence was all the confirmation he needed.

"I figured as much. What if he and his ex *are* back together?"

"If they are, it's my own fault," she murmured.

"Give me another chance, Shan. Please."

"No."

With his indirect attack a total failure, his expression darkened. "You're going to give up a sure thing that lasted for three years for the possibility of something that might never happen?"

Her first thought was to say that her relationship with Ty—whatever it was now—had no bearing whatsoever on her decision about Chris. Her second thought was to explain again why she couldn't be with him. Half a dozen other responses passed through her mind and were rejected. Finally, she said simply, "Yes, I am."

She pushed her chair back and stood. With one more glance at his handsome face, she strode toward the bar and asked June and Ben to box her dinner with an extra piece of prime rib. Ben quickly ducked into the kitchen but not before she caught the gleam of comprehension in his gray eyes.

Chris joined her beside the bar, and June and Luke moved off to give them space. "Shannon, come on. Think about this."

"I *have* thought about it." She turned to him while she waited for Ben to return with her dinner. "Tell me something, Chris. Would you have me take the movie deal or start looking for another teaching job?"

"You'd be happier teaching, wouldn't you?"

Before she could answer, Ben walked out of the kitchen and handed her a Styrofoam box that smelled delicious. She paid for her meal, bid June and Ben farewell for the evening, hugged Luke and wished him luck in the national championship, then started for the door.

"Shannon?" Chris asked, his voice trembling with uncertainty.

She met his gaze with a faint, apologetic smile. Relief lifted the weight of doubt from her as hazy inklings solidified into understanding. She inhaled deeply. "No, Chris, I wouldn't be happier teaching. If you knew me— truly knew me—you'd know that. Just like you should have known that tabloid article was a lie without needing to be told."

With that, she walked outside and physically and metaphorically left Chris firmly in her past. After Ty's cool reception yesterday morning, she had no idea if they had a future together or if they would be able to salvage their friendship, but she was damned sure going to find out.

* * *

Good lord it's cold today. Cold, gray, damp, and miserable, Ty thought as he took his gloves off and rubbed his hands together to warm them. He cupped them over his mouth and blew into them, but that did little to work feeling back into the tips. Of course, if he thought he was cold sitting astride his warm piebald mare after a vigorous workout, he needed to man up. His father sat in a cold wheel chair on the boardwalk on the south side of the pavilion's arena, rolling it back and forth to keep his blood pumping. He had to be freezing, but he'd watched Ty work Holly with a keen and critical eye and hadn't uttered a single complaint.

"She's definitely ready for that show next month. I can't wait to see the look on her old owner's face when he sees her." Hunter shook his head, grinning. "Damn, son, you sure do put your old man's skills to shame. Even as distracted as you are."

Ty met his father's probing gaze and abruptly looked away. "I'm not distracted."

"Horseshit."

Because he didn't want to be drawn into another conversation about Shannon, Ty stuffed his hands back into his gloves, settled them on his hips, and pressed his left heel to Holly's barrel while lifting his right. The paint mare obediently whirled around and around until he held both feet away, and then she stopped abruptly facing Hunter. Pride in her momentarily overwhelmed the uncertainty regarding Shannon, but even that didn't last long.

He braced his hands on his thighs and let his head fall. "You're right. I'm distracted."

"Shannon?"

"Who else?"

"You need to get your head on straight, Ty. Contrary to what your mother thinks, this isn't something that can be forced, so be patient and wait to see what happens. If it's meant to be, it will be. In the meantime, let's get in out of this cold."

Ty dismounted and strode to the big door on the end of the pavilion closest to the barn with Holly following faithfully behind and his father rolling along beside. He'd gradually reduced the level of exertion of her workout to start the cool down process, so the walk to her stall would be sufficient to finish it.

"I'm glad Heather wanted to stay on after she and you broke up," Hunter remarked. "You need a good hand to run this business, and since I'll never ride—or walk—again, I'm glad you have her."

Ty nodded. He imagined it would've been rather lonely training the horses by himself even with someone to take on the basic chores. With Heather assisting in the training end of things as well, he had a partner. For that reason alone, he would be sorely tempted to beg her to reconsider her aversion to domesticity if it turned out that

Shannon had indeed decided to go back to Chris. He winced with the thought of either of them settling for a mutually beneficial arrangement when it wasn't what either of their hearts truly wanted.

"I'm glad she's here, too," Ty murmured.

They entered the considerably warmer barn, and both sighed in relief. The woman in question was currently mucking out Shadow's stall with the colt tethered just outside and freshly groomed. She had also stoked the fire Ty had started this morning in the tack room's wood stove. She'd taken it upon herself to attend to the less glamorous chores while he'd been out in the pavilion all day to show Hunter how each horse in their barn was progressing with their training. Gratitude wafted through him. She *was* a good hand to have around, and a good friend.

When she noticed their arrival, she leaned out of the stall and grinned. "Don't tell me you boys are already tired of freezing your balls off out there."

"Yes, we are," Hunter replied without missing a beat. "Mine don't matter so much, but Ty might still have a use for his."

"He might indeed if he ever decides to get off his ass and do something about putting a ring on Shannon's finger."

Ty swore under his breath as his face heated uncomfortably even as his heart ached anew at the mention of Shannon. "You two are a pair of incorrigible tyrants."

That, among other things, was exactly why he and

Heather wouldn't have worked out. If he married her, he'd never come out of the barn in fear of the merciless and endless teasing she and his father liked to unleash on him. He led Holly into her stall and slid the door closed behind her, then turned his attention to Shadow. Even in the dim gray light filtering through the windows at either end of the barn and in each stall, the Arabian's black coat gleamed. When it was time to ship the young stud back to his owners in Washington in a few weeks, Ty was genuinely going to miss the beast. As if she sensed the direction of his thoughts, Holly reached her head over her stall door and nudged his shoulder.

"All right, kids," Hunter said. "I'm going to roll myself up to the house and get that show next month into the schedule and start making calls to get you in it, Ty. You *do* want to show Holly in it, correct?"

"That's right."

After bidding Heather farewell and thanking her for all her help around the place, Hunter left for the house. She stared after him.

"He still won't go for a power chair?"

"Nope. And every time someone tries to talk him into it, he just says he's got to keep what he has left in shape."

"He's a tough old bird, and I love him."

"Agreed, to both sentiments. It's been well over a year, and he's adjusted just fine. The rest of us…. We're still struggling with it."

"I suppose that's natural. It's a lot easier to deal

with the pain or injury or illness when it's your own, isn't it? When it's someone you love hurting… it's hard not to feel helpless."

She probably didn't mean to make him think of Shannon, but that's exactly who came to mind—that look on her face when she'd come back inside after talking to Chris. He'd wanted to take that pain away from her, but he couldn't, so he'd gone and made it worse by obeying the need to avenge it.

Needing something to do with his hands, he picked up a broom and swept up the litter of straw Heather had drizzled across the aisle of the barn mucking out Shadow's stall. His father thought he should wait to see what happened with Shannon, but his gut railed against that. He'd waited once before, for two years after he'd kissed her that first time, and now he couldn't help but wonder how different things might be if he had only acted on the same impulse that had driven him to do it. Would they be married now if he had?

He collected the pile of straw in a dustpan and dumped it in the wheelbarrow.

He couldn't wait again. If he did, he might lose her forever. At that thought, he straightened with an unfamiliar urgency and stowed the broom and dustpan, then turned to Heather to tell her he needed to go, but he saw by the knowing smile on her face that she already knew.

"Go get her, Ty," she murmured. "I'll finish up here."

"I'll make it up to you."

"Don't worry about that."

He strode down the aisle of the barn without pausing to acknowledge any of the horses that leaned over their stall doors to greet him as he passed. A whirlwind of tiny, wind-driven snowflakes swirled inside when he yanked the door open, and he smacked into a wall of bitterly cold air. Shivering, he shoved his gloved hands in his pockets, hugged his coat more tightly about him, and jogged down the driveway. He stoked the fire in his cabin to make sure it would be plenty cozy in his house when he returned home. Glancing at his watch while he waited for the larger logs to catch, he figured Shannon would still be at dinner with Chris at the Ramshorn. Good. Interrupting that would be the surest way to determine where he stood.

His gaze shifted to the Christmas tree he and Shannon had decorated, and that funny pain in his chest flared again. She'd been so adorable, and he'd hoped that it would be the first of many Christmases decorating the tree together, that maybe next year's wouldn't be his tree but theirs.

Might still be, he thought to reassure himself. He stepped over to plug in the lights, and one corner of his mouth lifted in hope. *It's not over until she says it is. Maybe not even then. Chris might screw up again.*

Satisfied that the fire was adequately devouring the wood, he closed the dampers. Still in his coat, he needed only to pull his gloves back on and head out the door. His stomach flip-flopped and his heart skipped more than a few beats with equal parts excitement and apprehension at the prospect of facing Shannon again. He tugged his cowboy hat onto his head and yanked the door open.

Shannon stood on the other side with one hand lifted to knock and the other holding a Styrofoam dinner box. Her eyes widened, and several moments passed before she lowered her hand. The apprehension on her face slammed straight to Ty's core, and were it not for the shock of seeing her *right there*, he would have given in to the impulse to reach for her and attempt to soothe it away.

It was another minute before she recovered her wits enough to speak, and when she did, she met his gaze head on, almost defiantly. He didn't have to wrack his brain to figure out what she meant because he'd been hoping to hear exactly those words since he'd ridden away from her yesterday morning.

"I get it now."

Eight

SHANNON COULDN'T REMEMBER ever dangling on a moment as precariously as she did now waiting for Ty's response. He knew exactly what she meant; that much was as clear in his expression as if he *had* said it out loud. But there was no hint of his reaction yet.

"So, you get it," he said at last, his voice quiet and deliberately even. "And you're still going to go back to Chris."

Never taking her eyes off him, she shook her head. "I told him to leave."

He still gave no discernable reaction. "Why?"

"Because he doesn't know me."

His brows drew together, and disappointment seeped over his features. Panicked, she floundered to find the right words that would explain everything she felt, but there was too much and it overwhelmed her. Coming up empty, she stepped inside and set the Styrofoam box on the small table just to the left of the door, knocking Ty's keys to the floor in her haste, and with a cringe of guilt for possibly betraying Heather, she kissed him. He straightened in surprise, but she threaded her arms around his neck so he couldn't escape. For one wrenching second, she thought he'd try, then he was kissing her back just as fiercely as she kissed him, and the tension that had been crushing her for two days disintegrated.

Giving in to the wildfire sensations that raced through her, she ripped her mittens off, tossed them to the floor, and clasped his face, angling her body against his. Feverishly, she unzipped his coat, peeled it over his shoulders and down his arms, encouraged when he co-operated and then helped her out of her parka. She pushed him back against the wall on the other side of the entryway. He grunted when he slammed into it but didn't relinquish her mouth. The urgency in his kiss and in the hands that gripped her waist was electrifying.

He slid his hands from her waist down over her hips and around to her rump, then hoisted her off the ground. Instinctively, she hugged his waist with her thighs like she might grip one of his horses, hooking her ankles as he pushed off the wall. He carried her into the living room and lowered her to the couch. Sitting as they were, she couldn't get close enough, but she was too wrapped up in the startling sensations coursing through her to care much. She'd had a few interludes with Chris so hot that all thought had been driven from her mind, but nothing quite like this. The urgency entwined with reverence and apology thrilled her.

With nothing but the Christmas tree and the fire writhing behind the glass in the wood stove to illuminate Ty's living room, the moment was rousingly sensual and romantic. She reached down to loosen the laces of her snow boots and kicked them off, then tackled his ropers. Pivoting so she straddled his waist, she pulled his thick wool sweater and the long-sleeved thermal shirt beneath over his head and pushed him down onto his back.

She'd seen more of him—all of him—that day they'd gone skinny dipping, but now she took in the contours of his naked upper body with an unfettered appreciation. Fervor deepened into wonder as she slid her fingertips over smooth bare skin, and finally, she found the words to express what she needed him to know.

"I'm falling in love with you, Tyger. Help me fall the rest of the way."

She leaned over him and reclaimed his mouth, fully intent on taking this all the way to his bed, but the demand left his caresses, and gently, he pushed her away. Confusion sliced through the haze of desire, and when he arched up to press a kiss to her lips with the kind of tenderness that would've made her melt any other time, irritation flared. She tried to coax him back into the fog of primal hunger, but he resisted. Frustrated, she sat back on her heels, but her annoyance quickly faded. The adoration in his eyes invited the same.

"I'm not in this for a one night stand or a wild affair, Shannon," he murmured. "If you want more, you're going to have to wait until you're all the way in love with me."

To anyone else, that might've been misconstrued as cockiness, but Shannon sensed the reason behind it. He respected her and wanted her to be sure before they did anything she might later come to regret. She pinched her burning eyes closed and chewed on her lips.

He sat up, lifted her into his lap with both her legs on one side of his, and leaned close to kiss her neck. Unlike their dance the other day, this time, he took his time to nuzzle the curve between her neck and shoulder. Tugging at the scooped V-neck of her sweater to uncover her shoulder, he smoothed his hand over her skin from her jaw all the way around her shoulder and down her arm to the fabric of her sweater, then followed his hand with his lips. With her eyes still closed to better focus on his caresses, she shivered.

"I was so afraid, Shy Eyes," he whispered, resting his cheek against her bare shoulder.

"Of what?"

"That my one chance with you was already over." His voice was a soft rumble that made her heart flutter, and when he skimmed his fingertips lightly over her arm, tingles of pleasure rippled through her. "I screwed up. I should've left Chris alone, but when you came in nearly in tears…. And then when you came to talk to me yesterday morning, I didn't give you a chance to explain. I'm sorry."

"I deserved that. I screwed up, too. I should have told him right then and there that we were done. I should've gone to you first."

They lapsed into silence, and nestled against Ty's chest with his arms folded comfortably around her, Shannon stared with unfocused eyes at the Christmas tree. Right then, it was like the last two days had never happened. Here she was with Ty, cozied up with him as if nothing had happened. It was an enormous relief to be with him; he was the perfect note to complete her harmony. While they'd been at odds, the chord had soured, stark evidence that she'd made the right choice in picking him.

"God, the last couple days have been awkward." She snorted. "And here I used to think things would be weird between us if I brought up that kiss under the mistletoe. I couldn't have been more wrong."

"I don't ever want us to be like that again," Ty agreed. "It's not like us to not be able to talk through our problems. Not that we've ever really had any."

"No, we haven't."

"Do you forgive me for giving in to my stupid male pride?"

"It wasn't stupid male pride, so there's nothing to forgive." She snorted. "Stupid is thinking I needed to have dinner with Chris tonight and feeling like I owed him an explanation of why I couldn't go back to him. I know what my brother went through with the bitch, so I understand what Chris must've felt when he saw that picture and read the article, and I felt somehow responsible even though none of it was my fault."

"You're not stupid at all. If anything, you're too giving and sweet. It's one of the many things I love about you—how willing you are to give people chances even when they probably don't deserve any. Out of curiosity, how'd it go?"

Abruptly, she jumped to her feet to retrieve her dinner. She handed it to Ty, and when he opened it, he regarded her with a brow lifted.

"It went *that* well, huh?"

"There wasn't much to say. And it was both much harder than I thought it would be… and in the end, much easier."

Ty walked into the kitchen and brought back two plates and accompanying silverware. "I get the harder part—you were with him for a long time—but how was it easier?"

With her fingers, she flopped the larger slab of prime rib on his plate. "You."

"I don't get it."

"After you rode off yesterday morning, it became pretty clear that there was no way I could keep you both in my life after this weekend, so I had to choose."

"And you chose me?"

"Without hesitation."

"Why?"

"Answer me this. Should I take the movie deal or go back to teaching? No explanation yet. Just answer the question." This wasn't for her benefit but his; she already knew what answer he would give, and he didn't disappoint.

"Take the movie deal."

"Okay, now tell me why."

"It's a gateway to what you really want—a record deal—and because you are in your element when you're on stage or singing or playing the piano or a flute or…." His voice trailed off, and he frowned. "What does that have to do with you and Chris or you and me?"

"I posed the same question to him, and he asked if I wouldn't be happier teaching. Because he doesn't know me." She kissed his lips lightly, smiling. "You do."

"Does that mean you're going to take the deal?"

"I don't know if I'm going to take *this* deal, because I think exploring this thing we've started here is more important, but I'll definitely take the next one."

"I've waited this long, Shy Eyes. I can wait a while longer while you go make a name for yourself on the silver screen or on the radio. Or both."

At the use of his nickname for her, she smiled. "Have I ever told you how much I love your name for me?"

"You have now."

He let her deepen the kiss, and when he dove after her neck much like he had when they'd danced but with less humor. The urgency returned, and she rotated toward him, their dinner forgotten. She leaned away to yank her sweater off, needing to feel his hands on her with a fierce desire that would have shocked her even a month ago. The wall between friends and lovers had been well and truly demolished.

"Shannon…" he groaned. "Our dinner's getting cold."

"Quit putting the brakes on, Tyger. I want this. I want *you*."

"I want you, too… but all of you. Body *and* heart with emphasis on the latter. I wasn't joking about that."

Directly contradicting his words, he grabbed her around the waist and rotated them both so they were lying on the couch with her on the bottom and the length of him on top of her. Then he nibbled all along her jaw, down her neck, and over her shoulder making comical scarfing sounds. She shrieked with laughter even as desire roared to life again. He held himself above her with his forearms resting on either side of her and his hands splayed behind her shoulder blades and grinned smugly. The playful gleam in his eyes and the way their edges crinkled in mirth added a delicious taste of the joy of their friendship, and she clasped his face to bring his head down so she could kiss him just as teasingly. If this marvelously multifaceted affection was what she had to look forward to, a life with him would be a never-ending song of laughter and love. That was a life she could embrace whole-heartedly and count herself blessed to have.

Maybe she didn't have so far left to fall as she'd

thought.

* * *

I'm falling in love with you, Ty. Help me fall the rest of the way.

The promise in that utterance saturated him, and if he'd ever heard sweeter words, he couldn't recall them.

The remnants of their dinner, which had been stone cold by the time they'd gotten around to eating it, still lay on the coffee table, but he was in no hurry to clear it away. Shannon had fallen asleep on him almost half an hour ago, stretched out with the length of her slender body over his with their limbs entwined, and though his arm was starting to ache from the weight of her head, he was in no hurry to rectify that, either.

They hadn't turned on the lights, but they had clicked on the radio, and Christmas music now played quietly from the small stereo on the end table between the couch and the wall. In the dim golden light of the fire and Christmas tree, his other senses were heightened, particularly his sense of touch. The warmth of her, the softness of her body, and the bumpiness of her cable-knit sweater captivated him as if he'd never felt such things before. He kissed the top of her head, inhaling the natural scent of her accented by the subtle fruity fragrance of her shampoo and the hint of pine, although maybe that came from the tree itself. The pretty little spruce had certainly added a wonderful freshness to his home. His gaze slid to the tree, and he smiled again as the memories of cutting and decorating it washed through him.

His father had been right. He'd feared he would lose her if he sat back and waited to see what happened, but that hadn't come to pass… and he hadn't needed to wait long, either. Still, the need to make sure she was certain of his intentions gnawed at him. Since him pushing for her to pursue a career in acting and music rather than teaching—more specifically encouraging her to do what made her happy—had apparently proven that he was worth taking a chance on, that would probably be a good place to start. Beginning with convincing her to sign the contract for the part in Kevin's movie. The offer was on the table, and while Kevin might offer another if she didn't take this one, that wasn't a guarantee. He couldn't let her throw this opportunity away, even if it meant she'd be gone from his life for large chunks of time again.

She shifted in her sleep, and he tightened his arms possessively around her. She might still have doubts about them, but he didn't. Now that he had her, he had no plans to let her go ever again. Whatever he had to do to prove that, he would, and if he had to rearrange his life so they could be together, so be it.

He jumped when the phone rang and quickly snatched the cordless off the end table near his head before it woke Shannon. Too late. With a yawn, she lifted her head and smiled sleepily.

"Hello?" he asked into the phone.

"Ty, it's Pat. I've been trying to get hold of Shannon for almost four hours now. Called her cabin, even stopped by, but she hasn't been home. Please tell me you've seen her."

"I have. She's right here and has been since about five-thirty."

Pat exhaled audibly, clearly relieved. "Good. I thought she might've gone for a drive to cool down and slid off the road or something like that. Chris came back a little after six, told me he'd be checking out in the morning, and said—and I quote—Shannon really is a whore."

"I'm guessing he'll be checking out a little sooner than tomorrow morning."

"He's already gone. And he's damned lucky it was Aelissm he said that to."

"I'll bet. You want to talk to your sister?"

"No, that's all right. I just needed to know she's safe. And I'm glad she's with you."

"Does that mean I have your approval?"

"You've always had it. To be honest, I'm surprised it took you two this long to get together. But maybe there's a reason why it didn't happen until now. Anyhow, I'd best let you go. The kids are in bed and Aelissm just gave me a rather sultry wink."

Ty chuckled. "Best not keep her waiting."

"Tell Shannon I love her. I'll talk to you both tomorrow."

After he ended the call, Ty set the cordless on the table.

"Pat?" Shannon asked.

"He was worried about you."

"Chris left already?"

"I don't think he was given a choice."

Shannon lowered her head to his shoulder again. What was she thinking? He didn't want to tell her what Chris had said, but he suspected she'd already guessed. He stroked his hand over her arm, both wishing she hadn't put her sweater back on and glad she had. He didn't need her silky skin or the feminine curves of her distracting him right now.

"I guess if you wait long enough, everyone reveals their true colors. I thought he was above being a petty ass, though."

"Why do you think he was a petty ass?"

"Pat and Aeli wouldn't have kicked him out if he'd been decent. Let me guess. He called me a slut."

"More or less. I'm sorry, Shy Eyes. You deserve better than that."

"Yes, I do." She tilted her face to his again and stretched her neck to kiss him. "Fortunately, I've found him. Or rather, I finally figured out he's been standing right in front of me this whole time. Why didn't we ever see it, Ty?"

"Maybe we weren't meant to," he replied, picking up her hand and twining their fingers together, "because we hadn't experienced enough of life to appreciate what we have."

"So, you're saying we were too young and foolish?"

"That's exactly what I'm saying. And it's not like we didn't recognize it *at all*. There were hints of it from the beginning. The skinny dipping incident sticks out in my mind. Do you have *any* idea how awkward that was for me?"

"Actually, I do. I spent the whole time trying not to blush. How about the kiss under the mistletoe? That was a pretty obvious clue, too. Not only that you kissed me but that I kissed you back."

"There are also all the flirty compliments of each other."

"Like me calling you Tyger and stud and you calling me beautiful and gorgeous. And Shy Eyes."

"Plus the covert glances to check each other out."

"Thinking the other was the sexiest, most amazing creature we'd ever seen." Laughing lightly, she smoothed her hand over his chest. "Looking back it was pretty obvious, wasn't it?"

"It really was."

"Well, I'm glad we've figured it out now."

She snuggled a little closer, and they settled into a quiet enjoyment of each other and the moment. Cozy fire, festive tree, snow swirling outside in a black December night, and the woman who had been at the center of his plans for the future for a lot longer than he'd realized…. It was a fairytale, and he prayed he wouldn't wake up to find that it was nothing more than the most incredibly lucid dream.

"Shannon?"

"Hmm?"

"You have to take the movie deal. Don't wait for the next one."

"No. I want to explore this—you and me—for a little while before I sign a contract that will take me away from you for months again."

"I'm not looking forward to being apart from you, either, but there may not be another deal after this one."

He dragged himself into a sitting position with his back resting on the arm of the couch and her in his lap facing the tree. In the glow of its lights, he saw her brows knit together. She inhaled to argue, so he cut her off with a kiss. When he released her mouth, amusement twisted her lips and sparkled in her eyes. What he wouldn't give to kiss her breathless… and much, much more. But not now.

"I know Kevin is a good friend of yours, but he's also a businessman who has invested a lot of time and money into your career, and if you turn down this role, he might think you'd turn down another, and he might cut his losses."

"I have to think about it."

"I'm beginning to feel like a broken record, but you've been thinking about it for weeks. What's left to consider? Say yes."

"What about us?"

"We'll make it work. We've been doing the long distance friendship for years now, so I'm sure we can make it work as a couple. Besides, we're both making a lot more money than we used to, so we can travel to see each other."

"I don't know…."

"Yes, you do. And if you don't, I do. I won't be the reason you don't go after your dreams."

"Why are you so thoughtful and considerate of me all the time?"

"I love you. When you're happy, it's infectious and I can't help but be happy for you and with you."

"I love you, too," she murmured. "As my best friend for sure, but more and more as, well, *more*. As everything."

* * *

The audition and waiting to find out whether or not the offer would come for the role should have been the most nerve-wracking aspects of the movie deal, but they weren't. Calling Macie to tell her that she was going to sign the contract as it stood had her stomach and knots and her heart bouncing erratically in her chest. She'd been able to put the phone call off for five days because Macie had been on vacation in the Caribbean, but she'd returned last night and had even called to ask Shannon if she'd made a decision yet. Like a coward, Shannon had said no, she hadn't. She had to do it today. With only six days left until she *had* to respond, she was out of time. Still, she'd put it off all day, jumping on the excuse of helping her brother and sister-in-law set up once again for a football game potluck at the Bedspread.

The plan was for her to call Macie as soon as the game was over. Ty had suggested she use the Bedspread's phone—an idea Pat and Aelissm were both amenable to—so she'd have the support she needed… and several people around who wouldn't let her back out of it.

The game thus far had been a thrilling one, as was fitting for a national championship, and she'd cheered the Bobcats and Luke as wildly as anyone else, but inside, she was trembling. Ty seemed so certain that they could make their relationship work around her schedule, as he'd been sure of everything else so far, so why couldn't she believe it?

It's too new. This idea of us together is too new and too soon after Chris. Too soon to be tested like that.

As if he'd sensed her inner turmoil, Ty reached for her hand and gave it a squeeze, and at once, her restless ponderings stilled. She folded her fingers with his and curled her other hand over both, then leaned her head on his shoulder.

The last seconds of the game ticked down with the Bobcats tied at fourteen, and with his imperturbably level-headedness and power, Luke found his receiver in the end zone and launched one of his signature Hail Mary passes. Everyone in the restaurant of the Bedspread leaned forward, sitting at the edges of their seats as the ball soared, and when the receiver plucked it out of the air, they jumped as one to their feet with hands in the air like the refs on the TV and cheered.

Shannon turned to Ty and threw her arms around his neck, glad to celebrate this incredible moment with him.

When the ruckus died down, Ty turned to her with a kindness in his eyes that made her knees wobble. "You ready for this?"

"It can't be that time already."

"It is."

"Can't I just watch the post game—"

"No."

"But what if Luke—"

"You can watch it later. Your brother recorded the whole thing, and he isn't planning to stop recording until the last of the post-game interviews are done. Remember?" He tucked her hair behind her ears and brushed his thumbs over her cheeks. "I thought you agreed this was what you wanted… so why are you still fighting it?"

"Because sometimes it's easier to linger in indecision. It's safe and familiar. Taking that irrevocable step—*any* irrevocable step—into the unknown is scary."

"Yeah, but once you take that step, you'll be relieved you did and wonder why you waited so long."

"You're not going to let me out of this, are you?"

"Nope."

With a shuddering sigh, she released him and wandered over to the end of the bar closest to the door into the kitchen. Pat was ready with the cordless. She snatched it from his hand, scowling when he offered her a placating smile.

"You might want to take it outside," he said. "It's loud even in the kitchen. Ty, you'd better go with her to make sure she does it."

"What am I, five?" she muttered

"They way you're hedging on this?" Pat asked.

"Yeah, that's about right."

Shannon stuck her tongue out at him, then hugged him because he was right. She wanted Ty beside her. With one last deep breath and taking Ty's hand to settle her racing pulse, she dialed Macie's number from memory and stepped out the side door while it rang. She didn't let go of Ty's hand, grateful for both the warmth of it against the snowy afternoon and the unwavering support.

"Shannon, what an unexpected delight," Macie greeted. "I hope you calling without notice on a Saturday means you have an answer for me."

"It does. Sorry for interrupting your weekend."

"I'm glad you did. What's the answer?"

"Yes."

"As is?"

"Yes."

"We have time yet to renegotiate for higher pay."

"No. The contract is generous enough."

"Come on, girl. We ladies have to fight for our equal share in this business. Kevin expects us to counter offer."

"I'm sure he does, and if it was anyone but him, I'd say go for it."

"If you're sure…."

"I am."

"I talked to him yesterday after I got back, and he said he'd talked to Chris, so I assume you've heard about the tabloid backtracking."

"I did hear."

"The new column goes to print on Monday. I'll mail you a copy as soon as I get my hands on one. I think you'll be pleased."

"Thanks, Macie. When will you tell Kevin?"

"Don't you think he'd rather hear it from you?"

"I suppose so."

"All right. I'll get the ball rolling on this. Do you think you could fly or drive out here this coming week or the next to sign the contract? Just so we can get this thing done and out of the way to free up focus on other things. That record producer friend of Kevin's—Gary Townsend at Jive Records—called while I was on vacation. He'd like to hear a demo of some of the songs you've written and recorded, and soon. I haven't called him back yet, but I assume you'd like me to."

"He's with *Jive*? Kevin didn't say which company he worked for, and I haven't had the time or the focus to look him up."

"I'll take that as a yes."

"Yes! Of course I want you to call him back! That's…. Wow."

With a few more pleasantries, they ended the call. Shannon stared at the cordless in her hand for almost a minute as the brevity of that one tidbit sank in. Kevin's friend wanted to hear a demo! Lifting her eyes to Ty's and seeing a spark of amused pride in them, she let out a tiny squeal, then threw her arms around his neck again. He hugged her tightly in return.

"I'm so proud of you," he whispered.

He could have cheered as loudly as he had when Luke's pass had clinched the national championship for the Bobcats and it wouldn't have been as powerful as that quiet utterance.

"Call Kevin," he added nearly as softly. "Then we'll go celebrate. Because you know everyone will want to join in. It's a big day for Northstar."

"I love this place," she murmured, knowing he was right. "And everyone in it. If things keep going like they are between us, I might just have to make Northstar my home base."

She didn't let thoughts of all the time she'd end up spending away from home—or, more importantly, away from Ty—if her career continued to head in this upward direction. She half expected him to ask her about her last comment, but to her relief, he didn't. It wasn't something she was ready to talk about yet, and in his patient, understanding way, he must've sensed that. She gave him another squeeze, then stepped away to call Kevin McNamara's personal cell phone.

"Shannon, my favorite songstress!" he greeted. "What a wonderful surprise. How are you?"

"I'm great, Kevin. Before you ask, Chris came out here, and he said he talked to you about the tabloid article. You didn't have to do that."

"Yes, I did. It made me sick to think something I did caused my beautiful starlet pain. I hope you two have worked things out."

"Actually we haven't."

"My condolences."

"It's okay. Things are looking up for me in that department." She glanced up at Ty, who watched her with a patient smile. "Way up."

"Do tell. Wait. Is it that cowboy friend of yours? The one who trains horses and taught you to ride?"

"That's the one."

"Oh, starlet, it makes my heart soar to hear that. I've always wondered…."

"You and half the world, apparently. We can gossip about it when I come home for a few days this week or next."

"Why are you coming home early? I thought you were staying in Montana until after New Years."

"I am, but I have some business to attend to that can't wait, and I think you'll like it."

Kevin gasped. "You're going to take the role?"

"I'm going to take the role," she confirmed, beaming.

Kevin crowed so exuberantly that she had to hold the phone away from her ear. His excitement was infectious, and in that moment, it struck her that, despite being such an astute and successful businessman, he had a delightfully childlike quality that endeared him to her and nearly everyone who met him. Maybe *that* was the key to his success. With Kevin's wonder, Ty's quiet confidence, her brother's gentle heart, and her father's musical spirit, she was surrounded by amazing, kind-hearted men, and it was clearer than ever that she and Chris never would have made it. The tabloid story hadn't doomed them; it had only sped up the demise of their relationship. She couldn't imagine him putting up with her being gone for the long stretches she would likely be, but Ty…. As he'd said, they'd already proven that distance wasn't a problem for them.

She bid farewell to Kevin with a promise to have lunch with him when she headed to Washington, responding with a noncommittal "we'll see" when the theatre mogul asked her to bring Ty so he could meet him.

"I'd love to go," Ty said after she ended the call. "And I'm sure I can rework my schedule to make room for a few days off. Heather can manage the training and chores while I'm gone."

"You say that now, but give Kevin just five minutes of your time, and by the end of it, he'll have you working for him."

"Hey, there's an idea. This movie's going to have horses, right? Do they need an extra horse wrangler?"

"I think they have one already," she replied, "but wouldn't that be fun? Maybe I'll ask him."

They laughed together. Then Ty's expression softened and he stroked his fingertips along her jaw.

"So… you feel better having said yes."

It wasn't a question, but she nodded anyhow. "Yes, you pushy, adorable snot, you were right. Is that what you wanted to hear?"

"I didn't want to hear anything, but the smile on your face right now is exactly what I wanted to see."

He dipped his head to kiss her, and she shivered.

"Cold?" he asked.

"If I am, I can't feel it." She kissed him again. "I'm way too warm inside right now to be bothered by the pesky cold."

Nine

AFTER THEIR DIZZYING TRIP to Washington, Shannon was relieved to embrace the peace of Northstar. She and Ty were arriving just in time to catch a breathtaking winter dusk. The same storm system that had pelted them with rain in Washington had blanketed the quiet ranching valley with almost a foot of fluffy snow. The fresh blue-white provided a lovely contrast to the pink, peach, and lavender of the Belt of Venus coloring the sky above the eastern peaks. Just two days before Christmas, most of the scattered houses glittered with Christmas lights, and Shannon felt like she'd stepped into a painting. In this perfect moment with the excitement of the past three days still burning brightly in her heart, she could very easily imagine coming home to Northstar to this and to Ty after a movie wrapped or a tour ended.

She snuck a glance at him as he drove up the valley. Affection for him coiled through and around her. Celeste had met him before, but it was with an entirely new eye that she'd inspected and gauged him. With a twinkling-eyed grin, she'd given Shannon her heartfelt approval of him. Macie had been quite taken with him, too, and Kevin had adored him. Shannon was fairly certain he'd wanted Ty as a horse wrangler on the movie even before he'd seen the man ride. After, he'd called the director, who had offered Ty the job on the spot base purely on Kevin's recommendation. It was only for assistant to the primary horse wrangler and it wouldn't pay as well as what he'd make from horses he would have trained during that period in his own operation on the ranch, but it would mean he and Shannon would get to be together for the entire shoot instead of several hundred miles apart. If the cut in income worried him, he'd given her no indication, and in fact, he seemed genuinely excited to try something new.

Shannon snorted. Regardless of her talent and his, this whole movie and their roles in the production of it were an example of nepotism at its finest. She wasn't going to complain, though, because it promised to be an incredible adventure and, as Ty had told her, might open a door to many more opportunities.

"You've been running your own show for a while now," she said. "Are you sure you don't mind playing second fiddle to another trainer?"

He shrugged. "Even if I hate it, it might drum up some more business for me for the ranch."

"Just making sure you still want to do it."

"You bet I do."

Without taking his eyes off the snow-packed road, he took her hand and pressed a kiss to her knuckles. She leaned over and kissed his cheek, then let the stunning scenery around them distract her.

As much as she was ready to be out of his truck, she *wasn't* in any hurry to part ways with him for even a few hours. After two nights sharing an uncomfortable hotel bed with Ty, she had no desire to spend the night alone. His cabin or hers, she didn't care, but since he had work to catch up on this evening and first thing tomorrow, his was the logical choice.

When he neared Elkhorn Road and switched on his right turn signal, she said, "Mind if we head straight to your house?"

"Why would I mind?"

"Maybe because I fully plan on spending the night."

"Do you, now?"

"Mmm-hmm."

"I might be persuaded to let that happen."

It had been almost two weeks since Luke's final football game, and in that time, she and Ty had spent very little time apart. She'd worked a few shifts at the Bedspread when Pat and Aelissm needed her to, just like old times, and spoiled their children absolutely rotten with several more horseback rides, more baking, and plenty of snowman-building, snowball fights, and sledding. All with Ty, of course, and often with *his* nieces and nephew joining them. Their courtship had been a whirlwind in terms of length, but they'd been friends for so long that it felt like they'd been dating much longer than they had. With each passing day, it had become more and more difficult to see herself spending her life with anyone else, and after this trip, it was almost impossible. If that wasn't love, then she didn't have a clue what was. Well, that wasn't entirely true. She knew now that it wasn't what she'd shared with Chris.

Thank God we didn't run into him. Since he worked for the same agency as Macie—that was how they'd met—it had been a real possibility. She might be over him, but she didn't think she was ready to face him again just yet.

Ty parked his truck below his house, and hand in hand, they climbed the steps up to the deck. He unlocked and opened the door, then lifted her hand over her head and twirled her into his arms.

"Welcome home, Shy Eyes."

"Mmm. I like that."

"You're still thinking about making Northstar your home base?"

"Not thinking about it," she corrected. "Decided on it. I love you, Ty, and this is where I want to be. Right here in Northstar. Right here in your arms."

With his eyes shining, he joked, "Do you really love

me, or are you just trying to get me into bed?"

Tucking her hands in his back pockets, she rose up on her toes and kissed him. "I really love you. All the way. How can I not? You're my best friend, and you know my heart better than I do." She gave a suggestive wiggle of her hips. "Mind you, I'm not saying I wouldn't love to get you into bed."

Chuckling, he pulled her inside and kicked the door closed. It was a bit chilly inside, so he stepped over to the wood stove to get a fire going, and she headed into the kitchen to fix some hot chocolate for them. Ty brought in their bags, plugging in the lights outside and on the tree on his way, and with that chore done, he checked his answering machine and called his father. All was quiet on the home front; Heather and Hunter and Danny had kept things running smooth as could be in his absence. Hunter had, of course, been informed of Ty's job on the movie within an hour after it had been offered and had already rearranged the training and show schedule around it. With the call on speakerphone, Shannon was able to hear both sides of the conversation between father and son, and the obvious pride in Hunter's voice made her heart light.

She had no doubt Ty would be every bit as great a dad as his father was. The image of him cradling his—no, *their*—newborn baby bounded gleefully into her mind's eye and quickened her heart. It also triggered an ache in other regions of her body, and she bit her lip to silence a plea to Ty to postpone dinner to practice baby making.

Settle down, girl. It's way *too soon to be thinking along those lines.*

The idea refused to go away, but she was able to ignore it and focus on her task. She poured the hot chocolate into two mugs and garnished them each with a candy cane—an old favorite of theirs since her first Christmas in Northstar nine years ago. While the house warmed up, they snuggled together on the couch under a quaint red-and-green plaid blanket and sipped their hot chocolate. They didn't talk—didn't need to. When their hot chocolate was gone and the house sufficiently warm, Shannon turned her attention to Ty. She was done taking no for an answer from him.

She twisted her body so she was lying on top of him, then slid her hands under his sweater and undershirt. His skin was hot against her fingers. Drawing herself up his body, she kissed his neck and daringly nipped at the angle of his jaw with her teeth. She waited for him to object again, but unlike before, he let her play. She stripped out of her sweater and tossed it to the side. Still he didn't object. Instead, he skimmed his hands over her bared skin, following his hands with his lips.

"You're not going to turn me down again?" she asked huskily. Goose bumps rose all over her skin, and tingles of pleasure coursed through her.

"Nope."

That single word ignited a firestorm, and boldly, she explored the lines of his body, demanding everything he had. With his arms behind her shoulders and knees, he lurched off the couch and carried her back into his bedroom, lowered her onto the bed, and yanked her boots and then her jeans off. After he unlaced his boots and kicked them off, she unbuckled his belt and unzipped his jeans. As soon as his boots were out of the way, she shimmied his pants down his long legs. She'd been waiting for this for a long time. Much longer than she'd realized, and now that the moment was here, she had no patience for foreplay.

"It feels like I've been waiting for this forever," he whispered hoarsely, echoing her thoughts.

She was already so lost in the sensations burning through her that she couldn't do more than nod in agreement. Their mouths met again, and they devoured each other as the same urgency that had infused their caresses the evening after her unfinished dinner with Chris returned ten times stronger. The last of their undergarments were shed in a rush, and annoyance flared. Crap. She wasn't on the pill, and they didn't have condoms. Trembling with raw need, she almost said to hell with it and the consequences. The prospect of pregnancy was far too appealing right then, but she couldn't bear the thought of the guilt Ty would undoubtedly heap on himself.

"Ty, we have to stop. We're not… *prepared.*"

He yanked open the drawer of his nightstand and pulled out a box of condoms. "Are you referring to these?"

She sighed in relief. "You've been expecting this?"

"I've just been waiting for you to say the words out loud."

"What words?"

"That you've fallen the rest of the way in love with me."

Again, she didn't respond with words. She snatched the box out of his hands, ripped a foil packet open, sheathed him herself, too impatient to sit back and wait for him to do it. She briefly considered taking top position, but decided against it. She wanted to be entirely at the mercy of the desire pounding in her veins, to submit to him as she'd submitted to the inevitability of this moment and every one that would follow.

"I want you, Ty," she growled. "Now."

Consumed by the same hunger that ached in her, he didn't hesitate. He pushed slowly into her, and she arched against him, spreading her legs and tilting her pelvis to take him deeper. The breath left her lungs in awe of this exquisite moment—a moment she hadn't conceived of until he'd kissed her under the mistletoe.

She didn't need to be warmed up; she was beyond ready, so she rocked her hips, cuing him to thrust faster and faster. So much for submitting. The orgasm built quickly with a breathtaking intensity, and she clawed toward it, digging her fingers into the meat of Ty's back until he gasped. It broke over her in shattering intensity and satisfaction, and she cried out, her entire body quaking with it. Ty braced himself over her, and his head fell as he panted for oxygen. He swore under his breath, and she grinned smugly.

"We've definitely and spectacularly crossed the line from friends to lovers now," she murmured breathlessly a few moments later.

Ty flopped onto the mattress beside her, his chest heaving. "Yes, we have."

Gradually, their breathing and pulses slowed, and he tucked her into his arms. The security and comfort she found there fulfilled her as completely as their lovemaking had ravaged her. It had been barely more than a month since Chris had broken up with her, but here she was, more deeply in love with her old friend Ty than she'd ever been with him. But didn't the best things always come when they were least expected? It was after a conference with a parent about his daughter's failing grades had left her in tears that she had called her former professor and mentor for advice, and he'd suggested she audition for that first play. Then, just when she'd settled into theatre life and decided to set her dreams of breaking into the music industry aside, Kevin had begged her to audition for the supporting role in his movie, and the contract for that had come the offer to put her in touch with his friend Gary Townsend. Now she was with Ty staring into a brilliant future filled with the same love and laughter that had laid the foundation of their long friendship. She hadn't been looking for any of the good things that had happened to her in the last few years; instead, they'd found her.

"We're going to have to start a tradition," Ty

murmured, skimming his fingertips over her arm.

"Oh?"

"Yep. Every year on Christmas Eve, we'll have to go up to the Bedspread for a kiss under the mistletoe to celebrate the anniversary of the first one. Starting tomorrow."

"I like that." Something tickled her consciousness, and when it popped clear, she giggled. "So, um, happy birthday a day early."

He laughed softly. "Thank you. Best birthday present ever."

"Oh, I can think of a few that might be even better."

"Impossible."

"Not even a baby?"

He propped himself up on his elbow and stared down at her, frowning. "Okay, that *would* be the most amazing birthday present, but that came out of nowhere. What on earth made you think of that?"

"Listening to you talking to your dad and thinking about how you'll be as great a father as he is. I haven't managed to get it out of my head, and it scares me a little… except that I can't imagine anything more perfect than having a baby with a husband who is my best friend. Don't your parents always say that marrying your best friend is the key to a long-lasting marriage?"

"Yes, they do."

"You still want me to be the one to help you with the whole family situation, don't you?" she asked, recalling that unexpected remark he'd made after their first ride with their older nieces and nephews.

"Now more than ever. I love you, Shy Eyes, and I can't imagine anyone ever making me as happy as you do." He kissed the tip of her nose. "But let's give you a chance to build your career a bit more before we start thinking seriously about babies, all right? When we're old and gray, I don't want you to look back with *any* regrets."

She pulled him back down beside her and draped her arm across his chest, smiling up at him. "Something tells me I wouldn't, with or without my career."

* * *

A quarter after three in the morning, a phone call announcing the imminent arrival of his newest nephew had jerked Ty out of what was the deepest, most satiated sleep he'd had in a long time. Shannon had offered to come with him to the hospital, but he'd told her to go back to sleep as it would likely be a few hours yet before April's baby made his debut. The boy had arrived just after six. It was now half past seven, and at the moment, Ty was sitting outside his sister's room and wishing Shannon was here while their parents and Danny's and the three older Fitzwater children ogled the new addition to the family.

As if his thoughts had summoned her, she turned the corner in the hall and stopped at the nurse's station to ask for directions to April's room.

"Good morning, Shy Eyes," Ty called, striding to her.

She greeted him with a hug and a kiss. "How goes it?"

"Fast. I'm an uncle again already."

"Oh, I missed it?"

"I'm afraid so. Come on in. The grandparents should all have had a chance to hold him by now."

"Have you?"

"Yep. Right after his mom and dad. He's beautiful and perfect."

"No surprise there. April and Danny do have quite a track record for making beautiful babies."

"Yes, they do." Thinking of what she'd said to them right after they'd made love, he nearly groaned. "I think we could give them a run for their money, though. But come on. Come meet my new nephew."

Ty took her hand and led her into April's room, pushing through family members on his way to his sister's bedside. April had regained her son and cradled him with a smug, possessive gleam in her eyes. As soon as she saw, Shannon, however, her grin widened into a warm welcome.

"Hey, baby boy, time to meet your Aunt Shannon."

Ty glanced sharply at his sister, who met his gaze with a tilt of her head and a sideways glance at Shannon as she handed her son to Ty's lover. He rolled his eyes, but he doubted that did a damned thing to hide either his shock or just how appealing the idea of making Shannon his nephew's aunt was.

"So, Shannon, I hear you spent the night with Ty

last night," April remarked a little too casually as she handed her son over.

"Yes, I did," Shannon replied, unbothered by the probe. "And I'm planning to spend tonight with him, too."

"Where did you hear that?" Ty demanded. "Because I sure as hell didn't say anything."

"Okay, I didn't *hear* it, but I had a hunch."

"Uh-huh. You gave birth less than two hours ago, but you're already back to business as usual."

"Ty, this is my fourth baby. It *is* business as usual."

Teasingly, he leaned over Shannon's shoulder and made a show of tickling under the baby's chin. "Don't listen to her, little guy. She didn't mean it the way it sounded. You're a very welcome addition to the family."

April stuck her tongue out at him.

"I haven't heard a name yet," Shannon remarked. "Have you picked one?"

"We *were* planning to name him Tyler after my brother like we named Hunter Daniel after his grandfather and father, but now we think it might be too much if they share a name *and* a birthday."

"Mmm. That might get confusing. What about Taylor? It's close but not too close."

"I like that," Danny said, striding into the room with breakfast for April.

"I do, too," April agreed. "Taylor Noel Fitzwater, since he was born on Christmas Eve."

"I thought Noel was a girl's name?" Danny asked.

"I said *nohl*, not *noh-el*. It's spelled the same, so on paper, it's still Christmassy, but pronounced like I said it, it's a male name. French I think. Do you have a problem with that?"

"No, ma'am."

Ty stepped back to give Shannon space with the baby. He sat on the bed beside his sister but couldn't take his eyes off his lover. *How strangely wonderful to apply that term to her.* The rapture on her face was possibly the most exquisite thing he'd ever seen. He'd thought she couldn't be more beautiful than she was when she sang or played… but this definitely rivaled that. He was so enamored that he barely noticed when April gently levered herself out of bed with her husband's assistance, nor did he pay much attention when the grandparents and bleary-eyed older Fitzwater children filed out of the room to go get breakfast. He was only aware that he and Shannon were alone… or almost with his sister in the bathroom and her husband out in the hall talking to one of the nurses.

"Marry me, Shy Eyes," he heard himself murmur. He blinked, stunned that the words had come out of his mouth.

She snapped her head up and met his gaze with round eyes. "Wh-what?"

"Marry me," he repeated more loudly, more sure of the words.

April and Danny returned before she could process his request, and with her face a mask of fondness, she handed Taylor to his father and made all the appropriate compliments to the new parents so as not to arouse their suspicion—a masterful actress. Still, when she slipped out of the room, Ty's sister looked at him with her brows drawn in confusion.

"Ty?"

He shook his head and followed Shannon out. He found her sitting in the chair he had so recently vacated, staring blankly ahead with her face worryingly pale.

"Shannon?" he asked cautiously.

"Did you really just ask me to marry you?"

"I think I did. I didn't mean to yet—I haven't even *started* looking for a ring. It just came out, but I know in my heart that it's right. I've known for a while now that I want to spend my life with you."

The pallor of her face terrified him. Had he misread her? Had he wanted this so much that he'd imagined more between them than there was? Had she not been fully honest when she'd said she loved him? No, that's not something she would be flippant about.

"I…" she started. "I can't. Not yet."

"I'm not asking you to marry me right here and now, Shy Eyes. I just want us both to know."

The shimmer of tears in her eyes when she lifted her head and met his gaze threatened to break him. "Ty, it's too soon."

"Maybe so, but how I feel about you isn't going to change no matter how long we're together."

"How can you be so sure?" Her voice broke.

"My heart has never steered me wrong. I love you. You said…." He clenched his jaw against the crushing force of heartbreak and disappointment, then forced himself to take a deep breath and respond calmly. "You said you loved me, too. So either you lied to me or you're lying to yourself."

"I didn't lie to you, Ty. I love you."

"Then say yes."

All that came out when she opened her mouth to reply was a tiny squeak. He saw the intent in her eyes before she acted, and when she whispered an apology and half-ran down the hall and out of the hospital, he couldn't muster the strength to follow. With his legs threatening to give out, he reached for the chair, bracing his hand on the back and feeling entirely fragile as he collapsed into it. He didn't make a sound, only rested his forearms on his thighs and let his head hang. He stared at the rainbow-flecked linoleum tiles, not really seeing them. Numbness stole the warmth from him, and he agonized over every memory he and Shannon had made over the last few weeks, and the only thing that contradicted their progress was Chris's visit. Was she not as over him as she thought? Did she still have strong enough feelings for him that she was considering going back to him after every reassurance she'd given Ty? He shook his head. No, that felt false. Shannon was at times indecisive and unsure of her own value, but she wasn't foolish. She'd put Chris behind her. Permanently. What was he missing?

It's too soon.

Maybe it was, but they could spend a decade more together and it wouldn't prove anything he didn't already know. Why couldn't she see it, too? With a strangled groan, he wrapped his hands around his head.

Time passed without him noticing, but it seemed like only moments before his parents and Danny's returned with their older grandchildren.

"Oh, sweet baby Jesus," his mother cried. "What happened? Is it April? The baby?"

He dropped his hands and shook his head wordlessly, unable to lift it yet. "April and Danny and Taylor are all perfectly fine and happy." He cringed when his traitorous voice cracked on the last word.

"Then what's wrong? Something's wrong or you wouldn't look like death warmed over. What happened, Tyler?"

"Shannon just snatched my heart out of my chest and ran off with it."

"What do you mean? Why would she—"

"Phoebe," Hunter said with the kind of quiet demand that commanded obedience. "Leave us alone for a few minutes, love."

His father parked his wheelchair in front of him, and Ty lifted his gaze to Hunter's concerned face, feeling like a boy of six rather than a man of twenty-six.

Twenty-seven, he corrected. *Happy friggin' birthday to me.*

"Care to tell me what happened?"

"I asked Shannon to marry me. It just popped out

when I saw her holding Taylor. She was so beautiful, Dad."

"I know that feeling well," Hunter said. "It hurts so wonderfully, but if you think it's strong when she's holding your nephew, just wait until she's holding your son. Or your daughter."

"Twist the knife a little more, Dad. I think there might be a few drops of blood left in my heart."

"Now's not the time to be melodramatic, Ty. If it hurts this much that she said no, she's the one. But I think *you* already know that. Now's the time to show *her*."

"She didn't exactly say no. She just said it's too soon."

"Is it?"

"Is it what?"

"Too soon."

"I…." He inhaled deeply, held it for a moment, then let it out slowly. "Not for me, but for her, maybe it is."

"I think you'd best find out."

"I didn't mean to ask, but last night, she started talking about babies, and then seeing her with Taylor just now…. Everything became so achingly clear, like I was staring at my future, and I wanted it so much that—"

"Ty."

The gentleness in Hunter's voice jerked Ty's attention to him. The opposing emotions of insecurity and conviction made his body quiver, and like the little boy he'd once been, he closed his mouth and waited for the piece of his father's wisdom that would fix all his problems as it had in his younger years.

"I know I've told you to wait and see what happens before," Hunter continued just as softly, "but this isn't one of those times. Go."

He didn't need to be told twice. He hugged his father and jogged out of the hospital, pondering the places she might have gone. His lips lifted in a determined smile. There was only one place she'd go in Northstar when she was upset—the only place with a piano.

* * *

Shannon parked her SUV in front of the Bedspread Inn but didn't immediately get out of the car. The sun had only recently peeked over the eastern peaks and now illuminated the Northstar Valley with the clearest, most brilliant white light. The fresh snow dazzled and muted the colors and contrast of the world, and even in her turmoil, the beauty of it awed her.

Her head was a discordant orchestra of conflicting thoughts and desires. She'd cried most of the forty-some mile drive from Devyn to Northstar as a thousand fears assaulted her. Was it too soon? How would they stay together when her career path would require her to be away for stretches of time? Would he be content to stand in the wings while she went out in pursuit of fame and riches? Would this dizzying, wonderful union be able to weather the storms that would surely come, or would it crumble like her relationship with Chris had at the first sign of real doubt?

Through it all, a single thought resounded over the cacophony.

I love him.

It was followed by another, less complimentary admission. She was an idiot. A month ago, she would have shrugged away the idea of marrying Ty, but their few weeks together had opened that door, and it wouldn't matter how hard she tried to close it, she couldn't even if she wanted to. And it was stupid to throw away something great just because she was afraid. Nothing in life was ever certain, but if she didn't take chances for fear of failing, failure was guaranteed.

She headed inside, opening the door carefully so the bell didn't jingle too loudly. Her hope that she might enter unnoticed went unfulfilled; Pat sat on the stone ledge around the massive hearth in the center of the room starting a fire. He smiled a greeting. She hoped her eyes had cleared enough from her crying enough that he wouldn't notice.

"I didn't expect to see you for hours yet. I thought you and Ty were going for a ride before our Christmas Eve dinner."

"We were, but April went into labor early this morning. She and Danny are proud parents again, of a little boy named Taylor. Mind if I play the piano?"

"Of course not."

She strode with a confidence she didn't feel to the piano, glancing at the beam where her brother and his wife always hung the mistletoe. The sight of that sprig of waxy green leaves and off-white berries tied with a bright red ribbon made her heart trip over itself. Glancing hastily away, she hurried to the piano and sat on the bench. She lifted the cover from the keys and flexed her fingers while she pondered what song to play. One that had first teased her in those days immediately following Chris's dismissal came to mind, and she held her hands over the keys for a moment more as she drew the song up from memory. Then the music flowed out of her, and seemingly with a will of their own, her fingers stroked the song to life. It was a quiet, understated tune with a touch of melancholy, but threads of hope tried to worm their way into it as thoughts of Ty cropped up. She shook her head and started over. When those hints of cozier emotions again appeared, she growled, stood, and snatched a pencil and a few blank music sheets from the compartment in the bench. Hastily, she scribbled the first verse and chorus of the original song and then played it.

There. That was the song she'd envisioned.

And yet, it wasn't right.

"It's beautiful," Pat said, leaning against the side of the piano. "But it's a little sad. I liked it better with those glimpses of joy. They made it feel hopeful."

She scooted over so he could sit with her.

"Maybe I'm in the mood for sad."

"Why? Everything's coming together for you in rather spectacular ways."

"Ty proposed."

Pat didn't seem too surprised, and she suspected

that what glimmer of shock he felt stemmed not from the news but her delivery of it. "The way you two have been acting around each other these last few weeks, I would've thought a proposal would be something to celebrate, not mourn."

"It is."

"But…?" He took the pencil from her and made the adjustments to include the happier notes that had popped in.

"It's too soon, isn't it?"

"Is it? You're talking to a man who *married* a woman barely six months after meeting her. You and Ty have only been pursuing a romantic relationship for a few weeks, but you've been friends for years, which means all you had to do was fall in love, and these infusions—" With the pencil's eraser, he tapped the notes he'd changed. "—tell me you have."

"But—"

"Have you heard me *once* say I wish Aeli and I had waited a little longer to get married?"

"No, I haven't."

"And you won't. If it's right, it's right, Shannon." He set the pencil down and rolled his shoulders before settling his hands over the keys. "Try it again. With me."

There was more to the song than what she'd written down, and when she came to it, Pat lifted his hands out of the way to let her play. This time, she didn't fight the music and let it envelope her.

The bell on the door jingled, and Pat got up to greet

his customers. She barely noticed, too absorbed by the song and how it was evolving from what had first come to her. Moments later, he joined her again, sitting with his back to the piano, but she didn't acknowledge him; she had to get the whole thing out.

After the last notes drifted into silence, she folded her hands in her lap and leaned back, satisfied. This time, the song felt right. There were words now, too, but she'd work on them later. "Well? What do you think?"

She glanced at Pat only to discover that it wasn't her brother who sat beside her.

It was Ty, and the tortured love in his eyes threatened to fracture her.

"It's the most achingly beautiful song I've yet heard you play."

His voice was so soft and tender that she was compelled to lean her head on his shoulder and hug him until the pain left his eyes.

She resisted. Barely.

"How did you find me so fast?"

Before the words were out of her mouth, she knew the answer. Even if he'd left within minutes after her—she assumed he would have made excuses to April for leaving—it would have taken him time to track her down. But he hadn't needed to stop by her cabin or her brother's; he'd known exactly where to find her. Because he *knew* her.

With that thought following on the heels of her brother's insight about the song, her doubts and fears fell silent. She searched his face, letting her eyes take in every cherished line and feature, and knew that she wanted to see that face every day for the rest of their lives.

"I'm sorry, Shy Eyes," he said. "I am. I'd take the words back until you're ready to hear them, but I can't."

"No, Tyger, you can't."

Aware that her brother and sister-in-law were watching with encouraging smiles, she took Ty's hand and led him around to the other side of the hearth for a little privacy. Flicking her gaze up, she pushed him back a couple steps until they were right under the mistletoe. Exactly where they'd stood two years ago today. Burying her hand in his hair, she dragged his mouth down to hers. The memory of that first kiss washed through her, and with faithful attention to detail, she replicated it, searching for and finding the same hesitant curiosity and the young desire that had stunned her then.

When she rocked back onto her heels, that memory was plain in his eyes, too, and the surprise was just as sweet as it had been that day—a wonder evoked by the presence of something much deeper than friendship. Only this time, this kiss revealed something richer yet.

"What was that for?"

"You *did* say you wanted this to become a tradition, didn't you?"

"I did." Understanding dawned as bright as a winter sunrise over his face. "Does this mean...?"

"Yes," she whispered, touching her lips to his

again. "Yes, I'll marry you."

He wrapped his arms around her thighs and lifted her off the ground, then spun around, and she squealed in surprise and joy.

"Now, *this* is the best birthday present ever."

She braced her arms on his shoulders with her hands curled around the back of his head. Thinking of their conversation last night, she laughed. "Nope. It's the best birthday present *yet*."

His laughter was deep and rich and brought a smile of the purest elation to her face.

"Hold me, oh, hold me again, cozy in the snow," she sang to the tune of her song.

In a voice she suddenly wished she'd heard more, he followed her lead and sang, "Kiss me, oh, kiss me again, under the mistletoe."

And she did.

Epilogue

"SORRY WE'RE LATE," Ty said as he and Shannon strolled into the Bedspread. He stomped the snow from his boots and shook it from his coat. "Looks like you all started the party without us, though."

"Since you *just* arrived home a couple hours ago, I think we can forgive your tardiness," Aelissm remarked, "but this is Northstar. You can't expect us to hold up the start of a party for too long."

"The thought never crossed my mind." Ty glanced around the restaurant. "You and Pat have outdone yourselves this year."

A bushy fir dominated the northwest corner of the room and looked like it had been decorated for a magazine shoot. Swags of pine and fir with festive red bows and shiny jingle bells graced the ornate Old West-style wall sconces on the eastern and western walls, and every table had fresh-cut evergreen centerpieces with red candles that added a cheerful glow against the snowy gloom outside. A giant wreath studded with lights covered a large section of the wall-length mirror behind the bar at the back of the restaurant, and there were glittering snowflakes and an assortment of ornaments everywhere. Ty glanced up at the beam where the mistletoe was usually hung, and sure enough, there it was. He glanced at his wife only to find she was a step ahead of him, grinning up at him and waiting patiently for him to catch up. Setting the bags of gifts on the floor, he took her face in his hands and kissed her soundly.

"That has to be one of the cutest traditions I've ever come across," June Conner said to her husband, who nodded in agreement.

"So, Ty, how was the show in Billings?" Danny asked.

Ty embraced each member of his family, who were gathered around the tables nearest the tree, before he answered. "Holly and I took first place. And guess who asked to buy her colt."

"Her former owner," his father replied.

"Yep."

"I hope you told him no."

"Of course I did. I'd never sell him to that man even if he weren't already spoken for."

"You sold him?" Shannon asked with

disappointment thick in her voice. She'd developed a particularly strong bond with the piebald colt from the moment she'd helped bring him into the world in February.

"Not exactly, but Holly's Yuletide is officially no longer my horse. He's yours, my love."

"What?"

"Merry Christmas, Shy Eyes. And, yes, I'm going to make you train him yourself."

She embraced him tightly. "Thank you."

"Considering the bond you two have already, I figured he'd be perfect for your first horse. The first one that's completely yours, anyhow."

She rewarded him with a kiss.

"It appears that we've already begun the gift-giving," Pat announced, "but may we pause for a moment to wish Ty and Shannon a happy first anniversary… even if it *is* a couple weeks after the fact. And also, I'd like to wish both Ty and Taylor a very happy birthday."

Cups of coffee, hot chocolate, and hot cider were lifted to toast those sentiments, and Ty's gaze wandered from one beloved face to the next. They were so fortunate to have such a warm, wonderful group of people to support them. Shannon's brother and his family were all accounted for along with Aelissm's grandparents, Marge and Roger. Shannon and Pat's parents and Ty's were also present, as were his sister and brother-in-law and their brood, the Conner family, Heather and her current boyfriend, and Celeste and her husband. It was a boisterous gathering, but he wouldn't have it any other way.

"All right, let's see it," Luke Conner said. "Because we already know about it."

"Know about what?" Shannon asked demurely.

"Your platinum record."

Grinning, Shannon reached into the largest bag Ty had brought in and pulled out the plaque with a platinum record commemorating her debut album selling a million copies. Though Ty had been with her at the presentation of it, it still awed him. The pride for her accomplishments was overwhelming.

"That is pretty damned amazing," his father said, choking up a little. He hugged his daughter-in-law. "We're all so proud of you, Shannon. Congratulations."

"Thank you. We have something for you and Phoebe and for everyone else."

She pulled out limited edition CDs of her Christmas single—the song she'd been playing two years ago when Ty had walked into the Bedspread thinking he was going to have to fight to convince her to marry him.

"CDs?" Ty's niece Emma asked skeptically. "Does anyone even listen to those anymore?"

"Well, you're going to have to because this isn't the version of the song I recorded with Ethan Gentry."

"Ethan Gentry," Iris O'Neil and Emma sighed.

"You're so lucky you got to work with him," Iris added.

Ty eyed Danny and Pat. When they caught him looking at them, he mouthed, *Already?*

Both men sighed.

"Yeah… he's great. Anyhow, this is the recording I did with Ty, and the only place you'll get to hear it is right here on these CDs."

"Ty? You did a recording?" his mother asked, stunned. "How precious for you two to have this!"

He nodded. "It's not as good as the single version, but Shannon says she likes it better. I'm not sure if she means it or if she's just humoring me."

"I mean it," she confirmed. "I keep trying to tell you that you have a great voice. Maybe not as powerful or dynamic as Ethan Gentry's, but I actually prefer it. It's pleasant and… soothing."

"That may just be you, Shy Eyes."

"Why don't you let the rest of us decide for ourselves?" Aelissm interrupted. She held her hand out. "Gimme mine. The rest of you, get off your butts and dance."

Ty pulled Shannon into his arms and struck a classic waltz pose, delighted when she beamed.

"So *this* is what you were up to while I was on tour this summer? Dance lessons?"

"Yep. Tracie and John were kind enough to humor me."

"Remind me to thank them."

The song started playing, and it once again sent shivers through him. She'd called it "Mistletoe Kisses," and it told a story of friends who became lovers after an innocent kiss under the mistletoe. Hearing his own voice coming from the stereo was decidedly unsettling, but he liked that Shannon enjoyed it.

"So, I have a present that's, um, just for you. And I leave it up to you whether or not to share it with everyone else because it's still early yet."

He tilted his head. "You have piqued my curiosity. What's the present?"

Her smile turned shy as she handed him the poster tube she'd carried in. He'd thought it was the signed movie poster from Kevin's film that his mother had asked for.

"I thought you said this was for my mom."

"It is. Sort of."

Without taking his eyes off her, he slid the rubber band off and unrolled the poster. It was printed on high-quality paper and laminated. At last, he pulled his gaze from his wife to see what it was. It *was* a movie poster… *sort of.* She'd taken their wedding kiss photo and turned it into a poster about a movie called *Baby, It's Hot Outside*, starring Tyler Hunter Evans and Shannon Marie Evans, coming in August. He stared dumbly at it, then shifted his gaze back to her. The way she had her lip caught in her teeth was so adorable that it momentarily distracted him. Then the meaning of the poster hit him so hard his knees went weak and he had to grab onto her shoulders to steady himself.

"Are you *serious*?"

She nodded. "Congratulations, daddy," she whispered.

He picked her up in a crushing hug. "Oh my God,

I love you, Shy Eyes."

Laughing, she replied, "Good. Because I love you, too."

"Well?" his mother asked. "What was it?"

Instead of answering, Ty handed the poster to his mother.

A moment later, she let out a shriek. "Oh my God! Sweet baby Jesus! I'm going to be a grandma again!"

Ty laughed, and soon everyone was laughing with him as Phoebe hopped around in her excitement.

"She acts like this is her first grandbaby instead of her fifth."

"It's her first from her son," his sister said. "Congrats to you both."

Shannon tilted her head up to him, pointing up. They were once again under the mistletoe. "To think," she murmured, "that all this started right here four years ago with an impulsive kiss."

With his heart soaring, he could only nod and kiss his wife. It had seemed like such a crazy, reckless impulse at the time, but looking back he saw that it was the smartest thing he'd done in his life.

Shannon smiled and sang softly, "Kiss me, oh, kiss me again, under the mistletoe."

* * * * *

Don't miss the next book in the
Northstar series:

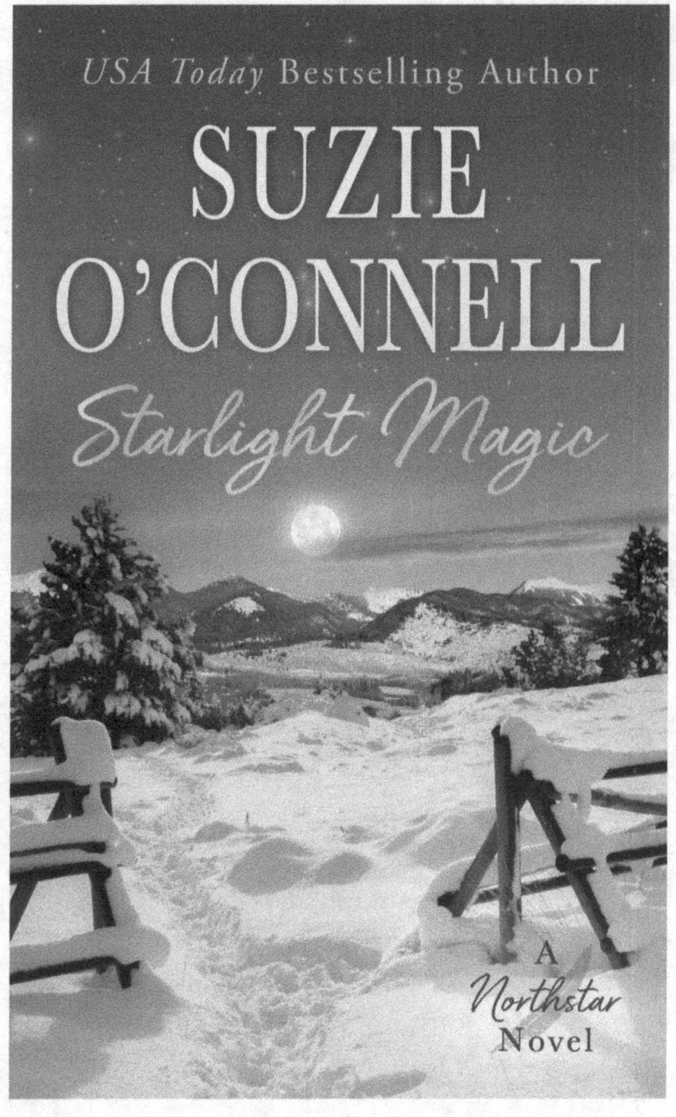

Starlight Magic

*Can the magic of the stars heal Celeste Dawson's tormented heart?
Single father Brodie Dunn will put his heart on the line to find out.*

Two months after her husband's violent death, Celeste is teetering on the edge, and she can't engage in the art that was once her escape from the world. She desperately needs a tranquil place to rebuild herself. An extended visit with her friend in Northstar will give her that… and her charming new neighbor might give her something even better.

Celeste is trouble Brodie doesn't need, but he's been where she is and he can't leave her alone to suffer. As he coaxes her out of the shadows, he discovers a heart as beautiful and mesmerizing as the stars. Celeste could be his perfect match, but will his apparent inability to take anything seriously drive her mad before he can prove it?

AVAILABLE NOW

Visit www.suzieoconnell.com for more information.

About the Author

Suzie O'Connell is the *USA Today* bestselling author of the Northstar romances. The series is the product of a love affair with Southwestern Montana that began with a two-week adventure at her stepsister's rustic cabin in her teens. That love affair shows no sign of abating.

She has been writing stories for as long as she can remember, and her love of writing and of Montana pushed her to earn a Bachelor of Arts in Literature and Writing from the University of Montana-Western. What else would you expect from a self-professed mountain-loving nerd?

When she isn't writing, you'll probably find Suzie in the mountains with a camera in hand and enjoying the beauty of Montana with her husband Mark, their daughter Maddie, and their golden retrievers Reilly and Angus.

Find Suzie online at www.suzieoconnell.com

www.ingramcontent.com/pod-product-compliance
Lightning Source LLC
Chambersburg PA
CBHW010346170726

48284CB00009B/2801